Crack the Spine

Winter 2014

Edited by Kerri Farrell Foley

This anthology is generously sponsored by Outskirts Press

ISBN-10: 0988978253
ISBN-13: 978-0-9889782-5-6

Library of Congress Control Number 2014900429

Published by Crack the Spine Press, LLC.
Printed in the United States of America.

Crack the Spine Press, LLC
Houston, Texas
Hattiesburg, Mississippi
www.crackthespinepress.com

CONTENTS

Puzzle Peace

"One Mary Eppstein, at 1530 Western Drive, was found dead today in her home. No foul play is suspected, but it took officers several hours to remove her body from the building due to what they would only call 'complications.' No one was allowed in to survey the scene other than police officials themselves. Chief Mallory said it was the policy of the Oakdale Police Department not to comment about ongoing investigations. She is not believed to have been a member of any anti-American skirmish organization."

The coastal skirmishes raged on, but Mary still looked forward to the arrival of her mail every day, as she had done for the last 25 years. As a child she remembered fondly joining her father on his daily treks down the long gravel road of their farm to the tiny silver box at the end of the drive. She would delight at the red arm sticking up, telling them that some sweet paper or packaged surprise lay within. Her father would reach in, sometimes simply pulling the mail out, but sometimes pretending that some unseen monster had grabbed his arm and was pulling him farther inside the mailbox because he knew this made her laugh.

Much like the postal service motto, there was no weather that prevented her from joining her father on the walk every day after lunch. When she got older and had to go to school, he waited for her to come home, met her at the mailbox, and they walked back to the house together, his boots and her shoes crunching across the gravelly surface while he flipped through the mystery envelopes.

On occasion, a box would come, but never for her. Brown parcel paper packages were always for her mother or her brother, but never for her and rarely for her father. He never seemed to mind, but Mary hated that nothing ever came for her. The joy of walking the distance to the mailbox was an elation that never wavered, even though she walked away from it disappointed every time. Her learning curve was nil. Soon, that joy was tempered; she enjoyed the walk more than the actual getting of mail.

Her father passed away. Her mother moved across the country to retire. Her brother went off to school and then enlisted. She lived alone in the house she had grown up in, had emptied it of most of its memories, made it her own. She repainted the walls, changed the locks, fixed faulty shingles in the roof, replaced aged doors that creaked with ones that swung on silent hinges. But she left the mail box the same shiny silver, a tiny glimmery beacon out on the edge of the property.

And then, seemingly out of nowhere, a package came, mysterious and brown-parcel normal on a sunlit afternoon.

Mary had never expected a package, having never received one before, so when the fat u-shaped opening was filled with the brown parcel paper, she gasped. It was a sound she'd rarely made and instantly she believed the package to be for someone other than her, for that's how it had always been. Perhaps the sender had not realized the other members of the family no longer lived here or no longer lived at all?

Her fingers slid beneath the parcel, pulled it out easily and scanned the ship-to label: "Mary Eppstein, 1530 Western Drive, Oakdale." No return address, no markings other than the sticker with her name and address on it. The package was, unbelievably, for her.

She ran her hands across the surface, feeling the rough paper crinkle beneath her touch. Her fingers trembled and her breath caught in her throat. It was beautiful because it was for her, had her name writ across it intentionally in firm pen strokes. The black ink was fluid and purposeful and held not a whit of hesitation. Someone had sent this to her and her alone and the thought was intoxicating. She held the package against her chest, feeling its hard corners dig into the folds of her arms and shoulders. Its flat bottom pressed against her bosom and she rested her chin on it, memorizing its shape before she held it out in front of her again.

The edges had been folded in and taped to the sides like triangles and a seam across the back showed the rough edges of a scissors' cut. She lifted it to her nose, sniffed the package, drank in its scent; paper, ink, woods, light glue, promise. So mesmerized by the package's smell, she hadn't realized that she had walked all the way back to her porch, smelling the thing the entire way back. She couldn't remember having even moved, couldn't remember even willing her legs to move, and yet…here she was, some fifty yards away from her mailbox and a foot away from stumbling into the lowest step of her porch.

Mary rushed inside the house, letting the storm door slam behind her, and had to stop herself from ripping the packaging to shreds so she could find out what mystery, what delightful gift, hid inside its paper folds. She sat on the couch and placed the package on her lap, ran her fingers around its circumference again, disbelieving. Finally, she allowed her slim finger to slide beneath the tape on the right side, unsticking it from the parcel and let the fold fall out. She did the same to the left side and felt her breath quicken, excited.

She flipped the package over and unfolded both flaps, letting the paper tear along the backside to reveal a shoebox the same color as the paper surrounding it, its former brand name faded into gibberish on all four sides. The lid was taped on and quickly she unstuck these, folding the tape up under the lid. Once lifted, Mary sat in silence and stared into the tissue lined package.

* * *

The next day, another package arrived. And the day after that and the day after that. Each new day brought another package, each addressed specifically to her with no return address, wrapped in the same parcel brown paper. There was never a note included, never a hint as to who had sent them, only what was written upon the objects inside.

The first box was full of pictures. Random pictures of people and places Mary had never known or visited. Each one had upon it one or two line notes attached that seemed unrelated to the images; daily devotionals from strangers with no return addresses and no

3

explanation, but all were somewhat cryptic in their own linguistically meandering way.

She remembered the first picture she pulled out. The picture itself was interesting enough: a pair of modestly skirted legs and old shoes in somewhere and during somewhen. It reminded her of childhood and Saturday sun-tastings, an innocence, a piety she could no longer run to, but it was the words splayed across the image that made her brain itch in the most pleasing of ways. The simplicity of the message complicated the meaning infinitely.

Four words: *"You are completely remarkable."*

It could be read a thousand ways with even more inflections possible, but brought more questions than Mary could answer. Was this some strange lover's ode to her? Did she have a secret admirer out in the shadows of the world? She flipped through the other photos in the box, hoping to find some clue as to the sender.

Images and phrases she found:

Footprints on a beach.
(You are missed.)

Sunspotted picnics with hard to see faces.
(I love that you love that I love you.)

A broken wall with graffiti across the bottom.
(Art will save us if we just let it touch our hurt.)

Skyscrapers that seemed to be touching the kingdom of clouds.
(I wonder what mistakes I made to lead me to this point?)

The rosy cheek of a baby (girl? boy?) and half of their lips.
(Living without you is my biggest fear.)

A teenager standing happily against a first car.
(Even knowing the now, I'd still make the same mistakes over again.)

Soda fountain store fronts with boarded up windows.
(My first job made me into the person I am today.)

A girl holding a flower in a meadow full of the same.
(Five years ago today, I said goodbye to you.)

Several pairs of colored socks strewn across a floor.
(No amount of outfits will ever change the me that I am.)

A tarnished trumpet lying in a drainage ditch.
(I gave up music to be with you; now I have nothing.)

A woman covered head-to-toe in mud, smiling. Laughing.
(One breast gone, one life left to live.)

An ocean at dawn.
(I miss our secret talks.)

Rush-hour on a bridge.
(How much of my life am I wasting every day?)

Cars picked clean and rusted over in a full junkyard.
(I have been dry for 13 years, but still fight the urge to drink every day.)

A woman crying into her hand while standing outside a burned down church.
(I am faith. I am love. I am invincible through Him.)

A sleeping infant on a sleeping man's chest.
(I love you bigger than the sky, deeper than the lowest sadness.)

A woman in tawdry fishnets sitting on a dirty Santa's lap.
(Remember when you gave me what I asked for?)

A boy in an astronaut's helmet, staring up into the dusky night sky.
(I wish I could remember all my dreams. They disappear by morning…)

Lawn gnomes and pink flamingos, seemingly at war with each other.
(At night, I pretend my lawn ornaments are the ones making all the noise so I
don't have to believe it's my parents.)

A pile of spent shell casings next to a child's sandaled foot.
(If we continue to fight around the children, the children will think it normal.)

Two nuns on a park bench, laughing, their robes pulled up to their knees.
(Breaking convention can sometimes be all you need to get through the day.)

A broken doll, a dirty jump rope, an unmade bed wearing tattered sheets.
(I don't remember the first or second foster home, but I wish I could forget the
last.)

Mary recognized no one in the pictures, recognized none of the locales, and yet still she felt herself splitting inside, cracking along each fissure, trembling both in delight and sadness as if she knew each of them personally. There was a truth to the photos and the words etched or written on them. It was as if someone had collected the hopes and dreams of a hundred people and sent them off to one (random?) person in the world to be shared.

She put the pictures back in the box and got up from the couch, clutching the box tightly as if it were a thing so fragile, so close to breaking.

* * *

Each day another package arrived, full of new photos and new phrases. Mary spent entire afternoons looking at the photos, reading the script across them, sometimes weeping long into the night. Rather than being an annoyance, these parcels had become an object of anticipation and excitement in an otherwise uneventful day, so it was hard to simply shrug them off as simply a weird occurrence. The writing on the ship-to label was always different, so Mary didn't think it could've been the same person anyway, oddity that it seemed to be. It was always one package, never more, over-postaged with two stamps in the upper right corner and a sticker of some sort along the back flap.

The packages were saved after the cards were removed and an entire room had been designed around the influx of one-liners and pictures now stuck in perfect patterns on the wall within. Another couple of inches all around and the room would be covered. Most of the images were clear and concise, but others were blurry or confusing and blotted out, but the words were what made the walk to the mailbox worth it every day. The red flag would go down on the metal container and a spring would find itself in each footstep closer to home as her eyes scanned every daily bit of linguistic art sent from who knew where and for what purpose, but the end result was always the same; a calm smile before bed and after waking.

On the fifth day, Mary took the photos and spread them across her guest bedroom floor, admiring the imperfection of each image. They were washed out or developed poorly, angled strange or too close to recognize the objects in the frame. Some were flimsy, some firm, some rippled with water from basement floodings or tears, and still others gleamed like new while many reflected nothing but age and crease.

With care, Mary began taping each image up on to the undecorated wall beside the fold out bed. One box of photos covered up a good section of wall and she began with another box, then another, then another, and finally the fifth. Her fingers graced the edges of the photos, left partial finger prints that she covered with tape and stuck to the wall easily. Side by side, they became a menagerie of memories, a flipbook of unknown faces and places with sentiment attached. Her wall had become the singular diary of a thousand strangers' voices.

She worked well into the morning. All five boxes had been affixed to the one wall with a few stragglers creeping over onto the adjoining one. She sat on the fold-out sofa and stared, letting her eyes rest on the arresting imagery, letting the words permeate her weary mind. The sun tinted the horizon beyond the window-shade, turned white into orange and she slipped into dreaming easily, falling asleep quick and quiet to a chorus of whispered voices she did not recognize.

After a full week of appearing parcels, she cleared out the garage and the guest bedroom. Once removed from the parcel, Mary taped each photo up on the wall of the guest room, none overlapping each other so that every bit of writing was visible. The first seven batches covered an entire wall. The empty boxes became a small stack in the garage.

This continued for a month. The empty boxes became a small wall of their own, stacked up against the garage wall neatly, like soldiers. Mary found herself liking the new aesthetic; the brown boxes calmed her thoughts the way the pictures inside them churned her emotions. By now, the guest bedroom had become full of pictures. The original wallpaper covered over completely, masked by the frozen moments of other people's lives. Not even a tiny glimpse of the wall could be seen behind the random visuals that now spread across the ceiling like the creeping fingers of a virus.

She removed all the furniture, stacking it up in her own bedroom, cramping the space so that she had to crawl over dresser drawers and recliner arms just to get into her bed at night, if she even made it to her own bed. Many nights she passed out in the middle of the guest room floor, staring up at the ceiling, itself now covered in pictures and text, with the latest emptied parcel spread out across the floor around her. Her sleep came while surrounded by Polaroids of the past.

* * *

Over the next several months, the coastal skirmishes had grown, moved inland, consuming cities as they moved. Had Mary gone outside to do her shopping, she would have noticed the increase in vagabonds and vagrants, refugees and displaced families moving into the area. The Midwest had become immediate sanctuary for those who chose no sides.

Instead, Mary had her groceries delivered to the house, leaving only to visit her mailbox. The packages kept arriving and she kept taping up image after image along her walls. The spare bedroom had shrunk; 144 square feet had become just a pathway into the middle of the room, a passage into an overload of sensory. It was just tall enough and just wide enough for her to step into sideways, but the images had spilled out and crawled along the hallway walls and ceiling like ivy. More pictures and furniture were removed, put into the master bedroom that had became a collection of personal belongings stacked up and nearly covering the bay window.

Her grocery deliveries shrunk; she was not eating. Mary spent all of her free time reading the cards over and over, shuffling through the house at one end and reading her way to the other, often never stopping to use the bathroom, itself covered in the word-scribbled images. Her once pink robe had turned a filthy pale and stunk of urine and glue. Her skin hung in limp folds beneath, gone grey from spending so much time in the darkness of burnt out light bulb hallways. She worried the heat from the bulbs would destroy the pictures she had come to need like the day's first meal, a drunk's first drink, or an after dinner cigarette followed by another and followed by another. The only light that came through the house found its way through the crevices of stacked furniture or tattered curtains. It shimmered and glinted off the surface of the pictures like dim starlight.

Had she paid more attention to the outside world, Mary would've noticed the droves of people clamoring across the countryside, their shoes barely considered as such and their skin smoke-blackened like refugees. Had she seen the waves of population filling up her town, she would've wondered who was sending the packages and why. She would've wondered what purpose the pictures had to someone else and why she had become the chosen caretaker for them all.

But she simply accepted the packages, absorbed the photos and their sometimes poetically vague maxims, cocooned herself within their very personal meanings. Her walls had shrunk faster than she had, but even now, she found it difficult to walk through the hallways and rooms. The thick barriers made of glossy paper forced her to suck in her stomach, will herself into thinness.

Sometime later, when a thin divot of hallway remained, Mary got stuck trying to move from one end of the house to the next. The pictures had finally grown too thick off the walls, imprisoned her, kept her immobile. She could feel the images burning against her, through her robe and then soaked up in her skin. Her eyes would roll up and over every glossy surface, drinking them in as she stood, wedged between the collected and wall-pasted pictures. Her chest constricted and left her with shallow breaths. She could look up or down, but not to either side. Her shoulder had pinned her in on the right, but she could wiggle her left foot. Unimaginably stuck and with no way to get herself out of the position. Statuesque and strangely calm.

Five minutes, twenty. An hour, three. Mary's sense of time disappeared with the wallpaper. She would feel the pictures tickle against her, each single edge itching against the bare skin peeking out from the robe. During the longer moments of impassibility, she would take to peeling off a single photo and nibbling at its edge to pass the time. She would graze on these new walls like a goat hungry to taste everything it saw.

She could taste the chemicals in the processed image, imagined the flavor of reds and blues, wondered about the caloric intake of yellow and the health benefits of black. The paper, rough-edged and indigestible, felt like stiff rock as she swallowed, scraping the lining of her throat before struggling down into her stomach.

Mary became full and by day's end, she stood wedged between her pictured walls unblinking and unmoving. Her throat had finally caught and prevented her from swallowing. She couldn't breathe and slowly, the lives that she had so decorously pasted up on her walls had taken hers from her.

Outside, the packages stopped arriving at the mailbox.

Only Human

Try being human
he said,

and figure out what
you want to say.

Get it half-written,
and type as if you had your hands
for one more hour,

as if they would be sold
across towns and labyrinths
and you never see your hands again.

Think about what you'd write
in the last hour you had your hands.

Write about losing your hands to writing,
then regaining them
in a battle for your hands,

the fight
to take back your hands,
to make them yours again,
and fold them together.
Hold your hand
in your other hand,
then point to yourself.

Hold your hands to your head
in the shape of a gun.

Hold yourself with your hands,
and lean on your hands.

keep the hands moving
in the same direction,

hold,
hug,
and fight back.

Write the story
for your hands
by your hands,

and sit up,

let the hands
wipe away the tears,

and lift
the body up.

Then wipe the palm clean,
start something new,
the truth.
Think
what it would be like

to write something new
with these hands,

all the words in the right order.

On This Day

The old man sitting nestled in the creek bed, displays the old revolver between his thin fingers. The revolver is a double action 38 Special, scratched and worn with a light brown handle and a barrel tinted yellow by the years. His stubbled chin trembles as he thinks of using it. When his chin does that, it usually means he's getting ready to weep. But, that's not going to happen on this day. He'll end those weak thoughts even if it means he puts the gun to his own head instead of someone else's.

It's approaching dusk, yet the heat still burns. Flecks of dirt stick to his damp skin. His pants are baggy and his belt is tight. He fixes his eyes on the creek in front of him. It's muddy. Autumn leaves float along in the watery muck, break free, and then stall in a clump at the base of a rotten log. He wants something to be clear, if not the creek, then something. He yearns for a crystal clear lake he once knew. He holds on dearly to the memories he can muster, lowers his eyelids and breathes deep. That lake glistened from a distance, yet it was even more majestic up close. When he waded in to his shoulders and directed his eyes to his feet, he could see his toes clearly like the water was barely even there. He swam to the center, ducked his head just under the surface and watched the cutthroat trout dart and play. Ripples of water circled from frogs splashing. The robust scent of lilies permeated the air. Back on the shore, he skipped stones across the shimmering surface; when the stones tired of skipping, he would lean in, squint, and watch them wiggle all the way to the bottom until they settled in for their endless rest.

With trepidation, he lifts his eyelids. He pinches the revolver with his thumb and forefinger by the tip of the barrel as if he's holding a mouse by its tail.

There is a ruffling sound above. He fixes his eyes on a white dove perched on a long twisted branch. "Pardon, you up there in the trees, I believe you're at least a thousand miles lost."

He waits for a response from the white dove. He waits some more before he decides it's best to go at him a different way. "I only think it's fair you know something. You best stay clear from me, my beautiful white dove, for someone's gonna get shot on this here day."

A dry breeze blows his white hair.

"Are you here to bring peace? I would not want to trouble you, but if you'd like, my beautiful white dove, could you bring peace to my sad heart? It's been oh so long since I've had any. For I'm sick, you see, and I need to get treated desperately." His voice shakes. "Or, I'll die."

The white dove tilts its head to one side and flaps its wings. The old man is pleased because he thinks it means the white dove understands him. Then, he knocks his head with his palm to clear his silly thoughts.

"This is not what a tough man does," he huffs. "A tough man would not talk to a dove and even if he did, he would not call that dove, my beautiful white dove. A tough man like I am today is required to be much more manly."

The white dove loves the old man. The white dove has admired the man's tenderness for all of the man's life. Even when the man was a child, he was a sweet boy. He never should have had to endure the abuse that was done to him, not as a boy, not ever. But, he remained good when others hadn't and that makes the white dove love him even more.

The old man trudges up the creek bank and presses his feet to the dry tickling grass. He searches his pants pockets and finds what he's looking for in the last pocket he checks. "There you are my new worst enemy. I will need you soon," he says to the gun.

He hears one wretched thing, his blood thumping in his ears. Thump. Thump. He worries his ears will burst and bleed out.

There's a little rundown gas station ahead. It dons wood siding that was plucked from the side of a barn. It's stained a deep gray and marred with tufts of black like a wolf's summer coat. A splintered

14

bench presses against the front wall. In the shade of the bench, a small straggly dog rests with her crooked ears poking straight out. Her pokey ears remind him of a dog he loved as a boy. She stirs up ancient memories of hurt and love and love and hurt all over again and how everyone in his life is either dis-interested or dead, well mostly dead. His chin scrunches up. He won't think of it anymore, not today.

He confronts the door. He notices a sign at eye level. In big block letters, it reads: No Shirt, No Shoes, No Entry. This throws him off. There are two rules on that sign, two rules he hadn't expected: wear a shirt and wear shoes. Well, these rules would have thrown him off yesterday, and the day before yesterday, and the day before that. But on this day, he's going to disregard the sign, the rules. He's going to throw caution to the wind, lift his chin, and step through that door. He'll place his feet ever so delicately on the floor so no one will notice his bare white feet and how he broke rule #2.

He palms the door lever and pushes it. The door shudders, but doesn't budge. He pushes it again, hard this time. It bangs. Still nothing. "What the?" he mumbles. He steps back, sits in front of the door with his legs crossed and studies it. The dog trots over, lies down in his lap, and licks his toes. He recoils in a stifled giggle and pats her wrinkled head. After a bit of time, the Pull sign stares at him. "Of course," he says, nodding his head. "The old Mr. Pull sign, my lifelong nemesis."

He prods the dog off his lap, rises up, and pulls that door hard. He sticks out his bottom jaw to look like a bulldog, because bulldogs look tough. He steps inside presenting an aura of pride that fills the room. Slap. Slap. His feet smack the floor. His pride vanishes. He gasps and curses his feet. "Damn you old feet. You forgot about rule #2."

He nervously scans the interior. No other customers are here. He glances at a row of a dozen kinds of beef jerky, and then directs his eyes to the counter. It's manned by a big burly clerk who's leaning forward, elbows on the counter, cigarette in hand. A haze of smoke hovers over him. He resembles a mountain, a big bad smoky mountain. The old man's eardrums bang. But, the fright dissipates some as he remembers he has the great equalizer in his pocket, an old 38. What a relief the clerk isn't some nice boy or some kind lady. He thinks perhaps it is acceptable to shoot him, because he looks like the criminals he's seen on TV. Then, he imagines the clerk deserves it. If he kills this man, he will be doing not only himself, but society a favor.

The clerk behind the counter spots a little old man making his way toward him. He waddles like a duck. His bare feet smack the floor. But, that's not all. He has forced out his lower jaw, so he looks like a deranged waddling bulldog. The clerk takes a long drag from his smoke and studies this strange new creature. He eyes the surveillance camera and winks. A strange cast of characters ramble into his den. The camera catches all of them, all of the fools. He revels being a brute on camera and spewing vitriol at the unsuspecting prey. On scheduled evenings, he gathers with his friends and plays the videos for them. He makes an event out of it, with cold beer and fried Buffalo wings. They laugh at the suckers who stumble into his lair, and he often replays their stupid antics to be viewed again as the room explodes in raucous laughter. This worthless old fool is promising to bring the most laughs yet.

"Where are your shoes?" The clerk roars in a deep gravelly voice. The old man freezes in place like he's playing the old Red Light Green Light game. His limbs are frozen in unnatural positions. Even his eyes are fixed. They're focused upon a white plastic sculpture on the counter. It depicts a garbed woman holding a young lifeless man stretched across her lap. On the base of it, a brass label reads, Pieta.

The burly clerk speaks loud and slow, "You're quite the old fool, aren't you?"

The old man remains frozen.

"Get over here," says the clerk as he blows on the red hot cherry tip of his smoke.

The old man is still frozen. He's not just frozen in motion, he is freezing cold from the air conditioning cranking out wintry gusts and blasting his thin hair and damp skin. Now, not only is his heart pounding in his ears, but a cold shiver crawls across his skin and seeps into his spine.

"Are you old and deaf?" the burly clerk rumbles.

"Sir?"

"Where are your shoes? You don't want me to ask you that again."

The old man spins on his heels, does a 180, and slaps his feet one after the other on the cold tiled floor toward the exit. He can't think of anything better in all the world than leaving this loud, freezing rundown filling station that's saturated with the stench of smoke and his own personal failure. He speeds to the exit and pulls on the door. It won't budge. He pulls again, hard. Nothing.

"Leaving is not an option for you, apparently." The clerk laughs with contempt.

"If I do what you say, will you unlock the door and let me out, my kind sir?"

"Do you really want me to answer that?"

The old man prepares to sulk. Then, he reminds himself why he's here. Last Sunday, he chose to live. He is strong today. He looks the clerk squarely in the eyes, pushes out his bottom jaw, and waddles to the counter.

With urgency, he searches his back pants pockets. He looks at the clerk quizzically. The burly clerk has the same curious expression the old man has, with one eyebrow raised and a subtle awkward tilt of the head. The old man snaps his fingers and pulls the revolver out of his pocket and holds its tip between his thumb and pointer finger.

"You're not here for a scratch ticket, are you?" asks the clerk.

"No, I have business."

He scans the clerk. He looks like an outlaw. His charcoal black mane is framed with strands of steely gray. His beard hangs heavy from his rugged face. He's probably never helped another soul in all his life. It will make his job easier when it comes to killing him, he reminds himself.

The old man raises the shaky revolver to the burly clerk's head. His finger is placed firmly on the trigger, begging for blood.

The clerk is strangely composed as he sizes up the danger. "Put your twitchy finger outside of the guard. You're likely to blow my brains across my treasured no smoking sign behind me." The clerk motions his thumb behind him while keeping his eyes on the old man, his lit cigarette hanging from the corner of his mouth.

The old man stands there befuddled, not quite believing he is where he is.

The clerk pinches the old man's trembling finger and extends it to the outside of the trigger guard where it's safer, but not safe.

The old man closes his eyes so tight they hurt. The gun dances in front of him. The clerk places the tip of his nose in the barrel. This steadies the revolver. The old man opens one eye. It has a tiny pool of tear on its lower lid.

The burly clerk whispers, "My wife loves this ugly bearded mug and I really think my daughter would miss my blueberry pancakes come Sunday morning."

The old man lowers the gun to the clerk's gut. "I came here to rob you and kill you."

"No, you didn't."

"Yes, I did. I really did," the old man says, almost sure of himself.

"No, you didn't," the clerk repeats flatly.

"I didn't?"

"You are deaf, aren't you?"

"Sir?"

"You didn't and you won't."

"But, I'm desperate and—"

"And what?"

"And the world is better off without mean people like you."

The old man raises the revolver to the clerk's heart, glares at him for a long time, way past being awkward, and then swings it up and points it at his own head. The clerk twists out his cigarette on the counter. The old man's finger tightens around the trigger, but his frail fingers are no match for the long heavy pull needed to move the hammer and ignite the round. In a single motion, the clerk snatches the revolver, thumbs the release, and disengages the cylinder. The ammunition sprays and clangs on the counter. His voice booms, "That's not going to happen here." He slams the old six-shooter on the counter.

The old man looks down at his toes and whispers, "Please, don't judge me. You don't know the terrible pain I live with."

The clerk's voice softens a little, "Well, that's not going to happen here."

The old man is broken, but not beaten. He raises his chin. "My kind sir, please call the police. My life is in your hands. Tell them I'm threatening you and that I'm tough," the old man pouts. "Don't you see, I'm sick. An emergency room won't do. I need ongoing treatment. Prison is my last option."

The burly clerk's heavy stare weighs on the old man's shoulders until they slump. "You don't know what you're talking about, do you?"

The old man stammers, "S-sir?"

"You don't know what you're talking about."

"You must not have heard. There doesn't seem to be the money, you see."

"You'd be lucky if you lasted one week in there."

"I know I won't last another week out here." The old man scans his deeply sun-spotted hands. He doesn't recognize his own aged skin anymore. He's scared. He strikes the counter with his fist. The ammo jingles. "I know it's no place for me!" Then, the old man checks himself back into the humility he's comfortable with and quiets his voice. "I know it's no place for me. Please, I wouldn't be here unless I had tried everything else." Meekly he asks, "You don't want me to die, do you?" His voice breaks. "If it be your will, I'll speak no more." He fights back his tears. His pink nose burns. He hates that feeling, but he fights through it so the tears won't come. Stop the tears, he tells himself. No tears on this day.

The burly clerk examines the old man from his bare white feet to his deeply creased sad face. He picks up the phone, dials, and speaks.

"Hey Josie, I'm being held up at the old filling station."

The old man releases a small smile. The clerk notices.

"I don't know. The man is old but he looks tough."

The old man whispers, "Like a bulldog."

The clerk allows a little smile. The old man smiles, too. Their eyes meet. Their souls meet, also.

He sees a sparkle of hope in the old man's eyes. "He looks tough like a bulldog." The clerk covers the phone. "They're comin', brother."

The old man is bursting. He can't plug up the dam anymore. He scrunches up his face and tears drip on his toes. He is so happy.

"It'll be ok, old fella." The clerk extends his bear-like paw, palm up. The old man hesitates, and then places his small hand in the clerk's.

The clerk pats the old man's hand. "I did as you asked. I know a few guys inside who will look after you."

The old man asks, "How'd you do that thing?"

"What thing?"

"How'd you get the gun from me and release the ammo in one fell swoop like magic?"

"How do you know it wasn't magic?" the clerk barks.

The old man is taken aback. The clerk waits a few seconds, then chuckles loud and free.

The old man chuckles, too. "You teased me like friends tease each other."

"I did."

"Thank you," says the old man sucking in his lips, overcome with joy. A little jittery, he grips the revolver. He examines it, consumed with wonder like a baby discovering his toes. He feels the weight of it in his hands, extends his arms straight out like he's seen actors do on TV. He aims it just to the right of the clerk, closes the wrong eye and says, "Perhaps, you'll teach me how to use this someday?"

"You closed the wrong eye and yes, someday I will."

A tall wiry cop rushes in from the back of the store, sees the old man with the revolver, fumbles for his shiny new pistol, finds it, and steadies it.

The clerk sees the cop. His mouth opens, his eyes widen, but no words come out and it's too late anyhow. The old man starts to turn his head to see what the clerk is worried about.

Bam. The white dove crashes into the window where the old man is standing. The old man turns his eyes toward the white dove. The dove struggles to fly with his newly broken wing. The old man wishes to help.

The cop aligns the sights to the back of the old man's head and squeezes the trigger. The pistol blasts. The old man doesn't hear it. He hasn't even seen the cop, because the white dove has drawn his attention to spare him the fright.

The burly clerk hurdles over the counter and stretches the old man's lifeless body across his lap. He embraces his friend while looking at his sweet thin face. He rocks back and forth, back and forth, very slowly, gently, like he's known the old man all his life and he knew this gesture to be the man's dying wish. He won't stop until the police make him stop, and that's not for an hour yet.

The old man, who no longer looks old, awakens nestled in a creek bed under a grove of blooming trees. The tree above him shows off the prettiest white flowers he's ever seen. A light wind swirls. The caress of a thousand breezy kisses delights his skin. The air around him is freshened by the drifting scent of lilacs. He surveys the crystal clear creek in front of him; the ebbs and flows and trickles harmonize with him, become him. He smiles as he realizes that he has gotten to see crystal clear water again. I'm a very lucky man, he thinks. Tranquility washes over him like a cool breeze at daybreak. He looks up in awe at the white flowers. He soaks them in, widens his eyes, and then splashes cold water from the creek on his face to make sure he's seeing what he thinks he's seeing. He grins widely and sustains his grin longer than he ever has.

"Hello, old friend. It's been a long time," cheers the man as he gazes into the trees above.

"Hello, old friend," says a sweet voice in the trees. "Do you remember me?"

"Where have you been?" the man asks, still smiling.

The beautiful white dove swoops, lifts, and dives throughout the trees with the purest of joy and splendor. The man marvels at his old friend. He places his hands on his heart. He can't stop grinning and doesn't want to.

The dove's voice quickens with excitement. "Would you like to play by the lake? The crystal clear one, with the frogs and the fish and the-"

"Yes, yes of course," the man agrees.

"Do you remember where it is?" asks the white dove.

"I'll show you the way," chirps the man as he springs up and dashes off like a rabbit across the green pasture speckled with wildflowers, toward the glistening lake with his beautiful white dove fluttering and spinning playfully by his side, on this day.

Guitarist

crushes of gapes
in an interlace of sweat.
i walked above them like a sultry key;
like the kind of knife they used
to cut open their fruit.

love was precious, perhaps,
but i could see it in almost every eye,
glistening with the impulse
for regret.

the string-sung songs
fluttered like febrile birds,
uncaged as they rippled,
scudding on young lakes of sighs.

the intimacy was as real
as the rut of a cat,
but in the morning, the rumpus
condensed into dewy pains.

people trickled off, sucked
by the walls of the same grey cubes,
while the sun poured its useless cures
on the ache of their bedraggled heads.
the music
would start up all over again,
and the screams and the frays
and the riffs.

there were too many of them,
the sad perky crowds,
blending together yet granular,
spread out across all that could be touched.

mine was a world of stung myths,
glimpsed under a few brief spotlights--
those beacons of the faun,
risen from the aftermath
of clock-numbed days.

Calling in Sick

roaches 3am
when rioted by light,
annihilate the myth
of a straight line.

rush hour, *per contra*,
holds no such bravado,
disavows the wild,
or even the purr of a cat.

unemployed pigeons
strut sans stress,
giddy on a surplus
of perches.

cars, *ab ovo*,
putter in queues,
marinating in engine broth,
corseted by cement.

the heads under the glass
earn their fuel
by approximating draft beasts:
oxen, sheep, swine,

even bureau-
rats.

claim your collar
and prop your face,
till it wraps around your conscience
and sinks in.

Performance Art

Everyone at Parsons called her The Romanian Girl, somehow with those air-born quotation marks, even those who knew her name; although, there were many who did not bother to know. She was not remarkable in classes and seemed to have few friends. The woman of mystery one of her classmates called her. That she seemed so self-contained and isolated, as if sealed in a glass Mason jar like some home preserved peaches, perversely made her more interesting, at least to some of her fellow art students. In a cosmopolitan city like New York, the students paradoxically did not seem all that blasé about identity.

"There must be a story there somehow," one of them said. "No one can be that remote from ordinary life, sequestered in art, so to speak."

"Without a social life, where would you get your content," said another.

"Out of your head, your imagination," said Robert Green.

Her early drawings were not exactly exceptional, although they were often better than average. She seemed not able to catch that certain human touch in the required life drawing class, for example. She was not able to humanize her models when she put them on the paper. Her work there was more cartoonish, in fact, and she seemed to know it. But there was something original, often witty, in her approach. Sometimes startling and jarringly ugly, on purpose, it would seem.

"Her doodles show imagination and they are very clever", said one of her classmates. "Maybe that should be her forte – graphic novelist. If she could just relax. She seems really uptight, always on edge. Maybe she has something to say in a narrative because her drawings are often so static. Or maybe she is the next Roy Lichtenstein hiding in our art classes."

"If she could just let loose in her art," said another one over coffee in the nearby Starbucks. "We don't see that yet."

"I would think that, coming from Romania behind the iron curtain and growing up under the thumb of the communists, she would have a lot to say, in fact," said another. "You know, Saul Steinberg who escaped from the Romanian Nazi wannabes, always called his homeland 'that sewer of a country' and never went back."

"Can't necessarily blame the poor girl for that," said another student. "I understand she has a mother still alive back there."

"I wonder how she got into Parsons. Or why she found Parsons," said Robert Green.

"New York City and Manhattan is the Mecca for the arts and the artist. Why not Parsons in the heart of this great metropolis. And we do like to be international, of course, so why not a talented Romanian in our midst. Consider the history of the founding of The New School – all those smart Jews escaping Nazi anti-Semitism and the killing," said Allen Jablonski.

"She is incredibly polite, actually," said Robert Green. "Over-polite. Hard to believe, in fact, that anyone could be so deferential."

"Maybe the obsequiousness is a kind of social mask," said a friend. "I find something about her expression that gives me a chill, sort of like Vlad, the Impaler. I wonder if she comes from Sibiu in Transylvania."

"Don't deal with stereotypes," said one of the group.

"Could be there is some hot fire in there behind the polite pretense, a masquerade. I guess it may be a smoldering sexiness. What do you think?" Robert Green asked the group.

"Well, if you want to find out why don't you ask her out, Robby? Find something to do where you both can be loose and informal. Who knows what you would find out about Ms Dracula," Robert's closest photographer student friend, Allen Jablonski, challenged.

"Possibly I will. You know that the city of Sibiu in Romania -- Transylvania even --was recently hailed as a cultural capital of Europe. I read that somewhere – maybe the travel section of the Sunday *Times*.

Perhaps she is working up a portfolio to ensure a triumphant return to her home town. Who would know what artistic depths there are below her cover, or what her ambitions are." Robert stuck out his lower lip in a parody of childish defiance. "Besides, I think she could be really hot!"

"Now you're talking my kind of language," said another one of the art students, a painter. "Wonder if she would pose nude if I asked her. She has great legs, thin but great. Boobs aren't much, though."

"She speaks English pretty well, I must say. Only a hint of an accent, although she uses some words and phrases that are just a little off-center."

"So how is your Romanian, then?" asked Robert Green.

"Who needs language when naked? Just get her nude, you beast," rejoined yet another one of the group. "Who needs the pretense of a painting?"

"I don't know about that plan," said one of the listeners. "I think it could be like making love to a pair of scissors. I might prefer being sequestered with a muff shot from *Penthouse* or to computer search of "naked women" on my Mac"

"A Mac being used to find the apple of experience sounds appropriate, I would venture," said yet another."The Garden of Eden on line. How sick."

"A Weiner moment, perhaps, if you are that much an exhibitionist," commented another of the students.

"Now you are all being gross and immature," said Robert Green. "You are spending too much time watching trashy movies or the video games made for those late teen age males. You all should be beyond that by now. Grow up."

"Well, then if you try for a date, wear a surgical mask and sterile rubber gloves. There might be a lot of blood-letting. Have you ever read about the last days of the Communist dictator of Romania and his wife? Bloody but farcical. The firing squad guys had to chase them around a compound in order to execute them both. Maybe it is in the culture. "

"What does all that have to do with Ms Caterina Georgescu?" Robert protested.

"I don't know, but what do we know about her Commie past. Or her family. Maybe they were part of the Red dictator's entourage. " Allen Jablonski offered an opinion.

"Don't let your Solidarity show, you Pole," put in Mickey Brennan in his exaggerated put-on party-time Irish accent.

"Oh, for Christ sakes. Let it go," said Robert. "I have work to do in the dark room and I have had enough of you guys. I am a serious art student and I am leaving this company of nerds."

This semi-raunchy males-only conversation actually made Bobby think about Caterina and to watch her more in the classes they shared. He noticed she did have great legs, but that she looked malnourished when she first came to class. Probably she did not have a totally healthy diet while growing up in Eastern Europe, he guessed. She had narrow shoulders, and seemed rather childishly flat-chested, thin – even anorexic.

Eventually, she had begun to change how she dressed. Robert wondered if she had found some second-hand shop. The kind of consignment place where the expensive MBA ladies of Wall Street recycled those fashions no longer on the cutting edge but still close enough to it to be sort of trendy. These clothes, sexy looking, made her look high-quality, he admitted to himself.

Her initial stooped posture, as though flinching from an anticipated blow, gradually changed. She began to straighten up as she gained confidence in her work. And showed new poise in the classroom. Robert thought her work was becoming more interesting even if not exactly original in concept.

In fact, one day when the class exercise was to critique each other's work, Robert suggested to her she might work on the light and dark contrasts of one of her more attention-grabbing pictures. It was the first real exchange he had had with her. She looked surprised that someone had spoken to her.

"What do you want?" she blurted. Her eyes looked up at him and then dropped to look at her hands. Her expression seemed to suggest that he had in some way insulted her. "I know what I am doing, and what do you want anyway?"

"Nothing. Nothing. Just trying to be of help. That is the point of peer evaluations. That is the way some workshops are run."

"I don't need it from you. Who are you, the teacher? Why aren't you up front then?"

Robert wondered if he should just back off. Her response seemed extreme as if in answer to some message in his comment that she heard but he did not. Why bother, he thought, because I have better things to do with my life that stir up these hostile responses. Then he had an epiphany. She was actually afraid. Her hands were shaking and perspiration glistened on her upper lip. She was terrified, in fact.

"It's okay," he said. "Your work is really very good. Sensitive portrayal of your subject matter, I think. Of course, I am just a student, but the instructor must like your perspective. I heard him say so earlier." Robert was fibbing. He had heard no such thing, but he also meant what he said about her work, and he thought this frightened girl could use some encouragement, even if it meant a little white lie. He decided to take the plunge.

"How about a cappuccino after class? There's a coffee shop nearby."

"Is it cheap?" she asked. "I have a limited budget."

"My treat. A good American male does not ask an attractive foreign visitor out for coffee and then go Dutch." He tried to smile reassuringly. "And call me Robby."

"What is 'Dutch'? A kind of coffee?" She looked perplexed. She also blushed a little, presumably at the compliment.

"No, no. Just a phrase meaning to pay for oneself. Don't ask me why we pin that arrangement on the Dutch, but it is a common expression here."

"Okay," she said. "Sounds good to me."

Robby thought to himself that his friendly overture seemed to have flipped a switch in this young woman to produce such a change of manner.

Later as they stood together at the counter waiting to be acknowledged and served, Robby asked, "Would you like a cookie or a muffin to go with the coffee?"

"Yes, please," she answered after a brief moment.

"Which?"

"A blueberry muffin," she pointed.

She began nibbling at the muffin as soon as the girl behind the counter put it out on a plate while getting the two coffees, and by the time they sat down, she had eaten half of it.

"You were hungry," commented Robby, and then was sorry he had said it, since she looked discomforted.

"Yes," she acknowledged. "Small breakfast."

"What do you have for breakfast?" he asked. "Got to start the day with an adequate breakfast," he added, beginning to feel nurturing like his mother.

"Tea, piece of toast, sometimes two. I have a limited budget."

"Not enough. Not enough. You need someone to take care of you." Robby said that before thinking about the implications.

"I can take care of myself, thank you," she retorted. "I have come to United States by myself to learn more about art and photography. I have learned English at school at home. I know what I need to do. I can make my way by myself. I know what I am doing."

"I am sure you do," Robby said. "I didn't mean to be insulting, but you should eat a healthy breakfast. I know it sounds trivial but you really should. Helps you think more clearly the rest of the day."

"Sure, sure." She gulped. Her eyes became shiny, he guessed, with unshed tears.

"I'll tell what," he said hurriedly, "I'll just get us both another muffin." He pushed himself back from the table and turned toward the counter. As he did so, he imagined he glimpsed her surveying him in a calculating way; however, when he returned with the two muffins he saw her dabbing at her eyes with her paper napkin. Poor thing, he first thought to himself. Then he thought about how attractive she really was when she was not being defensive or belligerent.

That notion surprised him.

"Here you go, Caterina," he said, handing her one of the muffins. He considered to himself, with surprise that is really the first time I have used her name. He liked the sound of it.

So there began his courting of her, as his grandparents might have called the process, but it was in the way young art students struggling in the big city would have to do it.

They began it by having her call him Robby and he calling her Cate.

"We have to do the first name thing since it is the truly American way," Robby first told her, and she agreed.

She told him about her life behind the iron curtain. Her father had been a insignificant functionary in the communist regime under Ceausescu. The collapse of that government had included her father who found himself suddenly not only without a good job but identified as one of the Ceausescu's minions, even though he had been minor. No firing squad for him, but at first no regular income either, and no respect. He had taken out his anger where he could, on his wife and daughter. Caterina told of hiding in a closet when her father, drunk on liquor he could ill afford, would beat her mother for no reason. If she made the mistake of being visible, he might also slap her, or worse. When he had died of a heart attack, she felt both relieved and bereft.

It was during this terrible adolescence, that Caterina decided that art would be her escape, and it would be art in America. She had studied English. It became a kind of religion for her, recitations of the American gospel, along with art, that kept her going.

It worked. She got into this American art school in the most important art center in the world, and earned her scholarship help. She escaped, she called it, and never wanted to go back.

Robby was impressed with this drive and this ambition. The knowledge made him even more motivated to help this young woman.

He realized that out of somewhere in his DNA had come a protective instinct.

They talked about their photography assignments together. Went out together to find subject matter. Argued about the right approaches. Even arranged to take some of the same classes. And they had coffee and muffins together. They even often met early before classes where Bobby insisted Caterina eat a hearty breakfast, although she often protested that she could not get that much down. He usually paid and she stopped protesting.

"Eat up, Cate," he would admonish.

Of course, his cash reserves were not that large. He had money from parents and he had a part-time job, babysitting a room full of dirt for the Dia Foundation. He would pull-up any random weeds that seemed to appear at times, seeded from the past when the top soil was actually out under the sun, and comb the surface when it got disturbed. He even had a short term position as an artist's assistant which meant that he filled-in the black outlines that the pop artist created with the flat colors as stipulated. As he worked at this task, he wondered who was the actual artist under these conditions. He even managed to alter the colors slightly and noticed that the bold-name artist either never noticed or really did not care.

When he told Caterina about his jobs, she laughed, which she had done rarely until they became intimate, he realized.

"Art is such a business here," she said. "The capitalist artist and the proletarian workers, and just who is creating the product and the value here, and who should get paid the most."

"And where is Karl Marx when we need him?" responded Robby.

"Do not joke about Marx," Caterina would say. "Many terrible things were done falsely in his name, but with economics he was right."

"Speaking of economics," Robby said, "how about economizing and you give up your room and move in with me in my apartment on Houston Street?"

"What a romantic proposition," Caterina responded.

"I just thought I would sneak the big question by you hidden in the practicality if you were not paying strict attention," he said. "So about it?"

"At the end of the month when my rent runs out, speaking of practicality," she said. "Gives us time to move what little I possess." He hugged her.

Where they had come was a surprise to him. Unplanned. He remembered the conversations with some of the other students about "the Romanian Girl" when they all were all relatively new students, and now "the Romanian girl" was going to live with him and they both seemed very happy. How about that, he thought. Will wonders never cease, he thought, something his father might have said. Was he becoming both his parents?

College work proceeded well for both of them. He had accelerated by taking more than the usual number of courses, since he wanted to move on from being a student. He graduated with his BFA a summer session and a semester before she did. She was more timid about her work and wanted more time for each course. She stayed on track. When he finished he got a job with a non-union construction group, started by young artists, in fact, who needed support while they worked on their art. Robby had become very proficient in wood working as part of his art training in sculpture, his other interest besides photography, and could turn out professional looking wood cabinetry and flooring, so he began to earn very good money. His group even put together a roof-top deck for Robert Redford's New York City *pied-a-terre*.

When he told Caterina about that job, she was impressed. "Oh, Robert Redford," she said. "What a hunk, I think you would say that word?"

"You could say that," Robby answered, feeling just a ridiculous twinge of jealously. "I saw him do Jay Gatsby, but he was not really the type. You couldn't imagine him inventing himself like Gatsby. Too Hollywood self-assured. The latest one is better. Hollywood just can't seem to stop with F. Scott. He would see the irony if he hadn't drunk himself to death. There *is* artistic life after death. How about that. The American way is to invent, or re-invent oneself. But why am I giving you a literary lesson."

"I am interested in the American Dream," said Cate. "And self-invention. Such an American thing."

And are you self-inventing, thought Robby, and then dismissed the thought as too negative about this young woman he had decided to love.

In his free time, since construction work could be organized to fit his other life, and although the artist construction team was in demand, he roamed the city, taking photographs and refining his primary art. He also went from small gallery to small gallery in the city and found places that would take his photographs for exhibit. He began to feel exhilarated by his successes.

He gave advice and help to Caterina who seemed now to welcome that creative assistance. Of course, that made him feel even more pleased with himself, not just because he was helping his lover, although that was important, but because it seemed a tribute to his talent.

Then that spring as Caterina neared her own graduation, she reminded him over a blueberry muffin and a cup of coffee near the school, where they often had had a midmorning snack between classes, that she had only a student visa and that it would expire when she got her BFA. He knew that, of course, but just had willed not to think about it.

Denial. Escapist. He noted to himself.

"We could get married," he said, also as unplanned as moving in together , but when he said it, it then seemed the most natural thing in the world.

Caterina did not seem surprised by the suggestion. "Yes, we could," she said.

So they did. At City Hall, with little ceremony, after sitting in an outer room while other couples went before them. No wedding gown; although some of the waiting couples were dressed as if they were in a large church wedding instead of in a rather Spartan municipal office. Such ones giggled and snuggled, but Robby and Caterina sat decorously, waiting their turn. On the other hand, Robby knew it was a big step, but suddenly Robby wanted to keep Caterina and this move seemed the way to do it.

Then they went to a restaurant with his parents who had come to the city for the occasion and arranged the after-wedding event. Cate had no relatives in attendance. Robby did not even know if she had communicated this move to her mother back in Romania. Somehow he did not think she had or he would have known. He also did not know what his suburban parents actually thought about this surprising move of their son's; however, his father had given him his late grandmother's diamond engagement ring for Cate. His father actually seemed quite taken by this addition to the family.

"Smart girl," he said, "and pretty." Even if she did wear stiletto-heeled boots to go hiking with them in the nearby state park.

"Inexperience with American hiking," his mother had added after that occasion.

"Good to put the jewelry to use," his father had said dryly about the ring, but then his father was more the muted type when it came to expressing emotions. His mother seconded the remark. Robby appreciated the family gesture and understood the inclusive significance behind it.

Then the happy couple went back to their life in the city, she to her final course work and he to his cabinetry and carpentry and photography and the occasional inclusion in gallery shows. The more of those in which he appeared, the more opportunities for inclusion seemed to turn up. He was even recognized by gallery owners and other artists with whom he appeared.

The green card now seemed the next step.

The application interview went smoothly. The interviewer seemed to respond positively to the young couple and they could provide all the answers about each other and their life together to show this was not just some convenient short term fiscal transaction of strangers. At the conclusion of the interrogation, this official even wished them, with a warm smile, a long and happy life together. It did not seem like a cold bureaucratic cross-examination at all.

"We put on a good show, did we not?" said Caterina as they left the building.

"A good show," agreed Robby, who did not really think that was the term he would have used, but forgave Caterina because of her still limited English vocabulary. He thought their performance was authentic. His was, he thought, and decided that hers had to be as well. How could it not be?

In the proper time, Caterina completed her work at Parsons and received her B. F. A. She had already begun to seek gallery exposure for her photographs and hoped having the degree in hand would help, but the people who had begun to take Robby's work did not seem that receptive to hers. She made the rounds with a portfolio, but found the usual polite answer – not quite right for us was often the response – to be disheartening, particularly in the light of Robby's building success.

Except that as Caterina grew more exasperated with her lack of recognition, she grew more impatient with what she said was the slowness of Robby's professional acknowledgment by the gallery world. He seemed content with the growing respect, but she thought that he was being taken advantage of by rapacious gallery owners. When something was sold, they took fifty percent of the price. He explained that was standard procedure.

"You just have to stand up for yourself, Robby. Demand more shows that feature you instead of letting them swamp you in the dreck of others without your talent. Stand up for yourself."

"Oh, come on. I'm still a relative new-comer. What can you expect?" He protested over the usual coffee and blueberry muffin one morning. "I am doing all right for someone in the early part of an art career."

"No you're not," she said. "You are just too innocent about the art business. Too green. Too *verde*, I guess we would say it in Romanian. Not just your name, I think, though it seems to be fitting."

"What, art for art's sake, but really art for money's sake?"

"Money goes with fame, and fame goes with exposure and publicity." Caterina pronounced with conviction. "And more fame gets more money and bigger gallery."

"Well, all right. You are entitled to your opinion. We just happen to disagree, and let's not fight. We don't fight in my family."

"We always did in mine back home." Caterina finished her muffin as if she were devouring an opponent. "Sometimes with blows, particularly from my father before he died. My mother and I had to stand up for our rights. I learned to punch back."

"We don't and so shall we just let it go for the moment. This is our first married fight, and I don't like it."

"People fight," Caterina asserted. "It is part of life."

"And someone has to win and someone has to lose," Robby said, "and then the air is poisoned." H reached across the table and patted her hand. "Poison, we don't need."

"So, how is married life?" asked Allen Jablonski.

"Yes," put in Mickey Brennan. "You recommend we try it?"

The three young men were sitting together in the coffee shop while Caterina was buying art supplies.. Only Robby had graduated, and the other two were also between classes. The three friends met occasionally, although not that often since Robby had finished his BFA and gotten married. Sometimes, Allen and Mickey helped with construction jobs if they had the time and needed a little extra cash.

"I like it.. You go home together to the same apartment, and the same double bed." Robby laughed. "You have breakfast together. You talk about art together."

"Don't be so cavalier about it," warned Mickey. "It all takes some romanticizing, you know, and marriage may make that even more essential."

"You old passionate Celt, you," said Robby.

"Have to be, even though the Irish thing goes against my Catholic school inhibited upbringing, particularly when it was, ironically, with Irish priests and nuns including some sickies. Now, if they had been

Italian priests and nuns at my school, it probably would have been a different culture, less fake puritanical."

"We three should all go out to a jazz place I know," said Allen. "You have Caterina, of course, and she needs exposure to that great American contribution to world music, authentic jazz. We two guys can hustle up dates."

"Dates? Dates? What are they? Out of the past, yet. But, yeah, I have been cultivating a dark eyed colleen from mafia country. You may remember her from school, Robby. Angela Rossi. We share the repressive parochial school experience. Gives us something to talk about before we go to bed." Mickey turned to Allen. " So, you really up for an evening of great music?"

"Give me a little time to work on it," Allen said. "I think I can get Sarah-Jane Templeton. Maybe you remember her, too, Robby. Good kid from upstate New York. Real rural, in fact. What she knows about love and sex she learned from watching horses, cows, and chicken procreate. And her art isn't Grandma Moses, don't let the hick name fool you."

"I'll talk to Cate. Right now she seems totally involved with some art project. She can be a monomaniac when it comes to perfecting her work. Workaholic, I guess you could say. Wanting to be a success can't be bad, but all work and no play makes a girl — what is the saying?" Robby smiled.

But the triple jazz excursion was not to be. It kept being shifted from date to date, primarily because Caterina seemed always to have something that she had to attend to. Robby was understanding because he knew the source of her driven nature. Otherwise things seemed normal, or as normal as things ever seemed to be with the "Romanian Girl."

Mickey and Allen gave up trying to pin down an evening. They got involved in their own final studies and preparing for the graduates' final exhibition, and with the two girls they had talked about when the night-out was first broached weeks before. Curious how for some the approach of graduation made those connections of greater consequence, as if commencement and the awarding of degrees might just sever links that had become important.

Came commencement and Mickey, Allen, Sarah-Jane, Angela, and Caterina graduated.

After partying together, and then after the usual thrashing around while trying to find what came next after receiving the degree, they all decided that they could not leave New York City, Mecca for the arts, right away. They all settled in at make-shift jobs, as Robby had done; although, he was one-up on them since his early graduation and minor successes at placing his work in galleys put him ahead somewhat in a professional way. There was also the increasing demand for his wood-working and carpentry skills.

Mickey and Angela got jobs as waiters, or servers, as the new non-gender specific terminology had it. The tips were good and it seemed as if they were somehow still in the swinging cosmopolitan world, even if the work was menial, and working together did have its social benefits. Allen got a position as a wine waiter, much to the surprise of his friends who did not know he had the expertise.

"Not hard to do," he said. "Read some books and magazines that give you talking points. Any quick learner can do it, particularly for dealing with the insecure recently rich of Wall Street who don't actually have a clue and don't want to appear stupid or naïve. The newly-minted aristocrats of Greenwich are such suckers."

Sarah-Jane took over the Dia dirt sitting with Robby's help, and started to bone up on the kind of mixed drinks that a bartender would be asked to make. Angela had told her that she was cute enough for a bartender's position that was going to open up at the restaurant where she and Mickey worked. "Just get rid of that upstate moral code, baby," she had added.

And Caterina told Robby one evening that she was going to San Francisco where she had been accepted at the Art Institute there for graduate study. "I am not going to be doing these silly jobs, like the others, and wait for a big recognition. . If I can't break in here in New York, I will go to the next best spot in U. S. and get an advanced degree in a really hip place. Psychedelic art. Maybe that would be better step, anyway. Lots of cutting edge art in San Francisco."

"And me?" asked Robby.

"So, what about you?" asked Mickey when Robby later told them about this sudden change in his situation.

Robby looked down into his coffee cup and played with the remnants of his blueberry muffin. He pushed the crumbs around on his plate with a wet index finger and ate them from his fingertip. "She's gone. She travels light. Just green card to carry her along. She said that I could get a divorce in New York State, I could go ahead and file or not. Made little difference to her, she said. If I want to pay, I could send the papers and she would sign, or not. I guess I will. It is quite cheap as these things go and I don't want something like that hanging over me. My father, ever the practical man, says I had better get one now, so in case I come into money and success, she can't claim half of it under New York State community property law. No other plans concerning her or me."

"Well, shit, man. What a bummer." Allen said. "Took you for a ride, got her green card, and moved on."

"That's more or less what she said. I turned out to be really a greenhorn when it comes to matters of the heart, I guess. Green in name and green in gullibility. Or verde, as she said, in Romanian. Real verde."

"Anything we can do?" asked Mickey. "Track her down? Betray her to the authorities? Make her life miserable in some way? She was high quality at putting on a show when it was needed. Got to credit her for that."

"What did you say recently about her inventing herself in the great American tradition?" said Allen. "She is going to become the hip San Francisco artist."

"And you know what is the capper? I was looking for some prints of mine for the next gallery show and they were gone from my files. Well, hey, I thought, that's funny, but I can always process more, but when I looked for the negatives, they were gone, too. Only thing I can figure is that she used those prints for a portfolio for her San Francisco Art Institute application, and took the negatives, too, so that I could never claim them for an exhibition of my work and show her up." Robby grimaced. "That is the real bummer. I was just verde," he said. "Pure verde."

"I don't know>" put in Mickey. "Maybe we just didn't quite understand precisely where the lady's artistic talent lay. I should say it was not actually painting or even photography, but in performance art. You know, sort of a Jim Dine or Claes Oldenburg event, bur on a personal performance level. Think of your courtship, marriage and coming divorce as a "Happening.""

"Better than just chalking it up as your introduction to the dog eat dog art world," said Allen. "And let this *Joy* Gatsby go her way."

"I guess I have to," agreed Robby. "No other choice. Green in name and green in life. It was nice while it lasted, ignorance is bliss, being *verde*. Sort of like the job I had filling in the lines created by that next Michelangelo I apprenticed with who has not made it yet. Dada, dada, dada."

"Give the Irishman the last word," Mickey said. "To kind of paraphrase Harold Rosenberg, the maker of artists, with a twist, 'life is a canvas on which to act.' "

"Actually, I think as the party of the second part, Caterina being the party of the first part, I should get the final last word," Robert said. "Because as serious entertainers, we must pay tribute to the skill we all saw, me particularly, in putting on her Performance Art production."

"Amen," said Mickey.

The Shoes Make the Woman

It is always a pair of shoes that gives you power—ruby slippers, your ticket home. Glass slippers, your ticket up. There is no pulling of the sword for you. No scraping of steel against rock. Your rite of passage is quieter, done under the shadow of a heavy gown.

They are gifted to you by another. A woman who has passed her prime. "This will give you power," she says, handling them with care, like a relic of old.

You take them eagerly, desperate for this new strength. You slip them on, and the horizon tilts, your center of gravity shifts. You teeter back and forth precariously, and you quickly realize that this is a whole new world now, yours to take, but only if you can stand up taller, stand up straighter, and walk with grace, thighs pressed tightly together.

Years later, when you retire them to the rack of yesterday, when your soles touch the ground again, you are reminded of the strength in your arches and how the earth, eager to greet you, rises up to meet you as you run.

What Happens When You Don't Just Run

No, you cannot tell him: *these days I'd still rather ride the train home, alone, than ask for help.* That for two years you've savored carrying your own suitcase, up flights of stairs and onto buses, even as you hated it, even as you sprinkled copious pinches of self-pity and loneliness over the entire thing and baked it.

His simple offer: too easy. No asking, no arm twisting. You didn't even have time to think of it first and fantasize about it.

Prioritize the body. Go towards the bathroom stall. Engage in the familiar struggle of rolling suitcase versus door in too cramped space, and who fucking designed all the airport bathrooms in the world anyway?

Above the toilet paper dispenser there is a ham sandwich in plastic, half-eaten, or half un-eaten. Don't feel like an intruder. Don't be ridiculous.

The text from ten minutes ago that's sending you to the toilet is this: *Can I pick you up from the airport tonight?*

Zero is how many times he's done this before. Three months is how long you've known him. The internet is how you met.

Move your makeup bag to your carry-on. Easy access. You're still insecure in that way.

Re-put up your hair. Don't waste time wishing you showered, it's too late, it's boarding time.

The plane.

Imagine: the naked intimacy of him, car curbside. You: exiting the terminal with rolling luggage. Unshaven, unshowered, unslept.

A short flight.

The fasten seatbelt sign reignites, the landing sneaks up and catches you, standing, unbelted in the plane bathroom. Applying makeup, frantic.

You can't rub concealer over the silver Honda that came two years before this one in the black sedan. (You don't love him yet, you don't know the exact brand of his car.) Two years ago and a different him: clean shaven, pale yellow shirt. You: squinting in bright white suburban sun. Tunnel vision, a small airport. Nothing mattered, except him playing drums on the steering wheel. Waiting, trunk open in anticipation.

Or: 1 year before he acquiesced. When it was you, sending text message offerings, driving to airports, picking him up against his discomfort. "It's no big deal," you said. Driving to his apartment in a violent rainstorm, afraid the downpour was punishment for your vulnerability.

Come back to your life.

You want to extend vacation by twelve hours. You want to become a different person for a day, call in sick to yourself. Imagine: throwing away obligation for one more night, letting him stay in your bed. But the idea leaves your mouth with a sickening sweet taste, like eating a packet of splenda on a dare.

You wrote back yes, though, in the other airport, between the bathroom and your gate. You will wheel your black, worn baggage out to the curb to meet him.

He has already seen you naked, but he should have to work harder to see you this revealed.

Daft

She's the crazy one in the family,
Nuts.
Never interested in your name,
always carries an extension cord.

Inevitably around uninvited, unexpected.
No remorse.
Pointing to the sky at the plane,
taming the tiger with her extension cord.

Incessantly rings my cell; ignore.
Redials.
Tells me the flowers are screaming to death,
hangs up to jump rope with her extension cord.

Rhythmic sways side to side as I climb in bed.
Goodnight.
Says my dreams are full of milk and honeybees,
plugs in the empty extension cord.

She gives me pop tarts for breakfast.

Chicken Gravy

A child stands in her yellow panties behind a sliding glass patio door, looking out into the street. There are no curbs, no bike paths. The white vertical blinds stick to her back in the humid house. She is flanked by a black dog, tongue out. His warm saliva drips on her toes. In one hand she holds a lidless Starbucks cup; the other palm is pressed against the door. On the crumbling tar outside there is a man. He's been walking—she's been watching him come up the street from far away—from where a smooth outcropping of Jasper makes a natural slide in the Hautamakis' yard at the end of the block—where their boys' yellow Caterpillar toys—the land-movers and bulldozers—lay at the bottom, wheels up, still spinning. The man is small. Far away.

She drops the cup and a thin woman flinches in the kitchen. Half an ounce of cold and creamed coffee lands on the carpet. The dog sniffs around the child's feet. His tongue lolls out to lap the dirty fibers around her toes, catching between them. She squeals and pulls her feet up, one and then the other. Outside, the man squints. He's seen her dancing. He looks down.

The thin woman stubs out a menthol and exhales on her way to the living room. "Gimme that," she says, batting at the cup on the floor. One arm is in a sling; the other hand is shaky. The cup flies out of her reach and she nearly topples, lunging after it. "Goddamn it," she says. The child puts both her feet down and steadies herself with both hands pressed on the door. Her eyes follow the woman and the cup for a moment, then turn to the man. He is closer now, and frowning.

"You whined for it," the woman says. She picks the cup up and tosses it onto a pile of the child's clothes on a recliner. "Then alls you did was spill it."

The dog leaves the child and bounds after the woman. Her legs are tan and wiry under cut-off jeans. His muzzle touches her leg—wet, and he snuffs. Her good hand comes down and smacks his black maw. Her hand is full of rings. He yips and backs off—then slinks away to the back bedroom. The child watches the dog for a moment, then looks up into the street. The man is nearly there. He has a beard, and carries something strapped to his chest.

A sing-song ringtone comes from the woman's jean shorts. She reaches in her back pocket, looks at the phone, and claps it to her ear.

"Where the fuck are you?" she asks it. She goes to the kitchen where her cigarettes are still on the counter in a green box. The child has memorized the sharp black corners and swoops of the brand on the front but can't read the letters. She only knows that the soft white sticks are not candy. They are full of that fluff that bloats in the wet grass, and something fibrous that sticks in her baby teeth and leaves a bad taste for days.

The woman puts a hand to her forehead, lifting her bangs. The phone is crooked between her cheek and shoulder.

"Chicken gravy," she says. "I said chicken goddamn gravy. Not mushroom soup. Not motherfucking cream of mushroom soup."

The child's nose touches the glass, and will leave a print. The man is right there, two yards away. He should start running at her now, arms outstretched, mouth open to yell or curled in a snarl. He ought to have a belt out maybe, or a wooden spoon. Her skin readies for the impact.

"Whatever," the woman says. She shoves the phone in her pocket. "Worthless."

He'll fling open the door, probably, and she might take a step back or two before falling on her butt. She'll keep her eyes shut tight and watch that field of purple bloom behind her lids, and go to that place in the dark, pulling the purple blossoms in close until it's over and she's in her room and the flowers will bloom on her skin, and that's how she'll know that it was real, that it had to happen, that it will always happen. There is always purple. The woman goes there too—her arms show the flowers, and green stems too, dotted with pinprick aphids.

The man stops. He doesn't pick up speed and doesn't rush up the steps and into the house.

He'll roar in her ear. He'll bite her cheek until it bleeds. He'll slap the cup or the cigarettes or the bath-puppet or whatever it is out of her hands. Her hands are empty now so he'll just grab them and twist them behind her back until her wrists crack.

She leans back, her palms rescinding a minute amount of pressure from the glass. If she leans too far forward, she'll go flying face-first onto the cinder-block steps when he forces open the door. She shifts and the white blinds shimmy on her shoulder blades.

The man lifts his hand.

The child sees now what is strapped to the man's chest. A baby boy, in a blue sleeper with yellow ducks, riding in some sort of bag. His eyes are squinched up against the late September wind, one fist curled like a fiddlehead fern to his lips.

The man's palm opens once, then closes. He repeats the gesture, then brings both his hands down and cups them under the rump of his riding son. He smiles.

The child watches him walk on from the corner of her eye. Swatches of red flannel, a dark beard, khaki shorts. Baby blue. Then he's at the side of the house out of her view.

In the kitchen the woman rifles through a drawer, cursing. A small yelp, a sharp intake of breath, a long sigh, and then nothing. The black dog slips out of one door and rounds the corner into another.

The child raises her hand to return the man's wave, but he is already gone.

Where We Go

At the river,
we walk the slow salt flats.
Generate mirages of meaning.

Wings flapping, our souls
flee like windup birds,
doomed to find grief
in the gallery of mirrors:

memories of foliage,
blended branches,
gossip from the forest,
the death of the trees.

Our Coming Happiness

Peel back the vanishing points, see

the red bench set down
in our melancholy margins of lawn.
Our new city, its boundaries, detours,
way-codes, raids for redemption,
thunder blood, arteries streaming control.

The last of our sentimental
storms trespassing
on our beach-house blooms
aglow in the dark.

See the rain go lower and slower,
no turn left unturned.

Narrow Escapes

Let's see let's see let's see let's see. What have we here? The good guys kill civilian families in Kabul. Altoona is in flames. You suddenly appear in the Self Improvement section of the branch library. The one with no lions out front. The Pope's selling rosaries and absolution on the Vatican Shopping Network. You can tune in right now. An apartment building explodes on the Northside of town. The markets crash. The landlord raises the rent. The Potomac overflows its storied banks. Brahms is imperiled in Texas. There's a traffic jam in Harlem that's backed up to Jackson Heights. Volcanic ashes ruin summer vacations. We retreat inside to tell stories with contrived endings. A good Q-tip is nowhere to be found. At the Paris fashion show, Moschino's striped pajamas of death are the hit of the runway. A voice says, "Quick. Duck in here." Against this backdrop, plot unfolds.

* * *

A familiar alley. A familiar night. The feeling of the barrel of a familiar handgun in the small of your back. The silence is broken by rhythmic impact and bounce of a rubber ball on a garage door. It echoes your heartbeat pulsing in the back of your throat. You know the familiar bark of watch dogs snapping taut their chain leashes. You know the buzzing flicker of a dim streetlight. You know a desperate scream. It may be your scream. You snap to it and find yourself sprinting down this alley. It is 2am, and you wonder why you know the time. Children play here. You hear a familiar growl behind you. You run for your life.

* * *

Something tells you that if you look back, something bad will happen. But something bad is already happening. You dare not look back you run as fast as you can you cannot breathe fast enough deeply enough your thighs burn your lungs burn your right side hurts like hell you stagger forward trying not to fall. Someone stands in a dark doorway. You cannot tell if it is a man or a woman. It may not even be human. "Quick," the voice says, "duck in here."

* * *

I need protection. I try to hire Two Guys and a Gun, but it is a full moon and they are all booked up. Fine time to hock my glock. I bend my arms at the elbow. I try in vain to protect my two faces from the hard rocks in an unlocked box of paradox. I watch you sprint through the glare in this alley ahead of me dropping hot rhymes (smallpox) like breadcrumbs (tick-tocks) thinking they will show you (vox humana counterplots) the way back (electric shocks) but knowing there is no way back (down by the docks).

* * *

I Chase Manhattan. You chase the dragon. I chase a shot of tequila with lime then salt then another shot. You chase your god. I chase your nightmare. You love me but you chase me down a hole in the cold, cold ground. Something's nipping at your heels. You dare not look back. I chase you.

* * *

I love your red heels, especially when everything else is black and white and shadows are long and your red heels look incandescent. "They hurt my feet," you say. "They make it hard to run when I am being chased." And I tell you I love the way they shape your legs. The alley changes. It is narrow and winding. There are shops but they are closed. You sprint impressively on the cobblestones. The alley becomes narrower and narrower with each bend. One red heel breaks, you turn your ankle. You hop and yank the other heel off. I listen to the rubbing of your nylons as you sprint again. You want to look back but know that will be fatal. You are both dead and alive. I am chasing you. Or maybe I stand in a dark doorway whispering, "Quick, duck in here."

* * *

"What's a white boy like you doing in a place like this?" she asks me. "I poured Coca-Cola in my brother's ear," I confess. "It made an ice cream float of his brains. Now I am chased by his ghost. That's an

54

eagle and a vulture. They will try to disembowel me. " "Quick," she says, "duck in here."

* * *

I run as fast as I can. I cannot breathe. I am chased by swine flu, avian flu, armadillo flu, Dunkin Donuts flu, and by contrabassoon flu. Everything in the world has a flu named after it, and they are all chasing me, a posse of flus hot on my trail. I am chased by genetically modified organisms and by radioactivity. I am chased by my own addictions. By the whole psychotic cosmos and, even worse, by nothing. I run in terror from mutated mitochondrial DNA growling and foaming at the mouth. "Let it catch you," you say calmly, "there is no escape!" Then you whisper, " Let me tell you a story. You will change."

* * *

You are stuck in this alley of recollections where stories are ghosts and ghosts are stories. I am both dead and alive. You wear red heels. You show thigh and lean against the tomb of Lady Macbeth. "Hey mister, got a light?" you ask as I run toward you. Then you see what's chasing me. "Quick," you say, "duck in here."

* * *

You run as fast as you can down the alley trying not to pitch forward. "There must be an end," you tell yourself. But it is not in sight. You question what you think you know. Your journey seemed so full of awe and wonder, of love and being loved, of motherhood and rising bread. So how did it come to throwing rocks through windows of your house and boiling your children and feeding them to their father and being chased by devils. The compulsion to look back overwhelms you. "Quick," someone says, "duck in here."

* * *

"Quick," a voice says, "duck in here." I do. A demon shoos me through a desiccated metaphor that may be the door of you. The door is dried and the paint peels. But light shines through a crack. "That's my story," you say. On the other side of the door is another alley, another scream. Inside your story I am both dead and alive.

You are stuffed in a coffin and sawed in half. One half is dead. The other half is alive. You think this may be an ill-conceived self improvement book. You wonder if you'll ever need your red heels again. I love you but I lower you into the cold, cold ground. "I am half alive," you shout, but no sound comes out. "Hmmm," you think, "maybe I will need those red heels after all." You hope it is all just a bad dream. "Quick," a voice says, "duck in here."

* * *

"Quick," I tell you, "duck in here. If you tell me your story, I'll tell you mine." "Buy me a drink first," you say. You start somewhere in the middle and I cannot tell if you are moving toward the beginning or the end. I start to tell you my story while you are still telling yours. I am both alive and dead. If you read me, you change me. If I name you, I change you. We tell our stories as we run. We resist the compulsion to look back. My story chases your story. Your story tells my story a story. These stories never end. We just abandon them. And then we tell another.

"Quick, duck in here."

Aaron

Aaron:

plagues are such strange things
swimming through you, an unearthly,
multi-limbed creature with slow dances in its arms.

take my two youngest, for example
my boys, my babies. one day they played
with strange fire, unlike what my brother saw flaming
within a bush, this blaze had no holiness
about it, and so God burnt up them up,
like paper dolls. with their ashes
i daubed up my eyes and moved on.

that's the nature of plagues
to arrive unbidden, a sad relative
who comes to die upon you, the air
sour with their breath.

there was the time we both saw it coming
with our tribes angry, driven to go back
where there was meat and work,
a sacrifice to simple gods--earrings
and a sprinkle of blood.
their cries spanned the desert floor,
rose up to heaven. then we felt it,
the wind's changing, the sick smell,

saw everyone crumpling into
fetal position, arms flailing like newborns,
the bodies falling, slow and beautiful as the sea.

and i stood there in between the living and dead,
arms outspread: a broken symbol of atonement,
blessing all. my sons' faces wavered
before me like a mirage.
when i reached out to caress their cheeks
one last time, that's when
the rains came, God's weeping,
a father's rage at watching children turn and turn,
blowing away like dust.

Stranger in My Own Home

Owen sat in the top-floor corner office of the Winnis Building, his family's company's headquarters. The office belonged to his brother Caspar—or "Cap," as he always called him—the company's CEO. Out of one bank of windows, there was a view of William Penn atop City Hall, nestled in the midst of the Center City towers, and on the other side, the Delaware River waterfront.

"You'll really like the job I have lined up for you," Cap said, smiling.

Owen grimaced and shook his head. "You don't think my appearance—eye patch and all—will detract from my credibility?"

He had barely survived a bombing three months earlier at the National Museum of Catalonia in Barcelona. He was left with a badly damaged right eye, a cracked skull, and a shattered right tibia. The Spanish surgeons had put pins in his leg and operated on his eye, trying to save it. He spent weeks in a Barcelona hospital, unconscious most of the time, as they nursed him into a stable enough condition to ship him back home to the States.

"Not a problem, bucko. The eye patch is actually a key factor in naming you as vice president."

"Really," Owen said, sarcastically, anticipating a joke at his own expense.

"The board totally agrees with me. The eye patch, goatee, and crutch make you look exactly like a pirate, which gives you added cachet in the world of international shipping."

They both laughed.

Owen's chuckle was brief and stiff, since he hadn't laughed in months. The spike in blood pressure forced a stabbing pain to shoot through his eye and into his head, piercing the protective cushion of painkillers, then disappearing as quickly as it had come. Nonetheless, it felt good to let loose a little, just like old times.

He was always amazed that, even after being separated from his brother for months, the camaraderie and friendship came flooding back as soon as they got together again. One time, he hadn't seen Cap in nearly two years, and they both showed up at their cousin's wedding in exactly the same new suit. They were so different, yet at times had this telepathic connection, like twins.

"That's right, mateys!" Owen said with an exaggerated pirate accent. "Accept our trade proposal or we'll pinch your fleet."

"All you need now is a few blackened teeth and a parrot," Cap said, laughing even more.

"Peg Leg Winnis, they call me."

Their laughter ended suddenly, possibly because the subject—his crippling limitations since the bombing—wasn't particularly funny.

Cap stood up. "Let me show you your office suite."

Owen grabbed the arm of the chair and winced as he stood. He grabbed his crutch—a black metal cane with a brace at mid arm—and steadied himself before following.

Owen walked down the hallway a few steps behind Cap. Even without a bum leg, he had always found it difficult to keep up with his older brother, who was nearly a head taller and the more athletic of the two. Cap had been a champion running back for the University of Pennsylvania football team. He still ran five miles a day.

"How's the leg feel with the cast off?" Cap asked.

"Sore. And the doc told me I'll never play soccer again."

Cap corrected him. "You never did play soccer."

"I know." Owen shook his head dourly. "But now I've really got to let go of the dream."

Cap laughed as he continued down the hall.

"Seriously, though, the doc said that after a couple more rounds of surgery, I'll walk with only a slight limp."

Cap stopped and put one arm around Owen and hugged him. "This is really a raw deal for you."

"The leg will always be gimpy, and the eye is legally blind."

"At least you're still alive."

"I can look forward to a long, miserable life."

"You'll get better."

They arrived at a corner office about half the size of Cap's, with a view of the river and New Jersey. The oil tanks out of the other side were partly concealed by vertical blinds.

Owen looked around. It was a little too nicely appointed. "So you want me to head up the international division?"

"You'll be great, with all of the international economic and political analyses you've been writing over the years. You're a recognized authority and an expert in a number of cultures and languages."

"How about my political viewpoint?" Owen gave him a challenging grin. "Not exactly in line with company policy."

Cap smiled patronizingly. "They don't care. You're a Winnis."

"What are the key issues?"

"The same as for all international shipping companies today—the threat of terrorism. Security problems."

"We had that ship attacked in Bahrain."

"Tied to al-Qaeda." Cap shook his head. "Another key issue is retaining our number one client," he added.

"U.S. defense contracts?"

"Government economic-consulting contracts."

"In developing countries?"

"Improving their economies with international trade."

"Particularly trade with the U.S."

"Mainly."

"Sounds like CIA stuff."

Cap shook his head and frowned. Then he nodded reluctantly. "Maybe a little. Anyway, Owen, you'll learn the business quickly."

Owen hobbled over and gazed out of the bank of windows at the river, swollen with spring rains. A mothballed battleship was docked permanently on the other side.

He thought about his life goals—to explore the globe and share his observations about humanity, good and bad, with the world. Nothing more than wishful thinking at this point.

He turned back to Cap. "I don't know, bro."

Cap frowned. "You don't know?"

"My life's been turned upside down recently. I'm rethinking everything."

"I know that," Cap said, engaging him directly, firmly, as if negotiating a government contract. "And this job will be a great way to get a new footing."

Owen shook his head. "I'm not sure what I want to do."

Cap paused for a second and suddenly lightened up. "Oh, I get it. This has to do with that woman. What's her name? Ronnie Krane? Come on, Owen. Are you really going to wander around the globe looking for her? There are other women out there."

Owen looked down, studying the sight of his injured leg leaning weakly against his crutch. He knew he would never get used to thinking of himself as a lame man.

"I know what that's like, Owen. You'll get over her soon enough."

Owen wondered how he could have been so stupid. At first, when she never visited him or even left a message at the Barcelona hospital, Owen was worried. He thought she must have been injured in the blast. Then, when he found that she was not on the casualty list, the concern in his stomach soured into anger, first at the world for messing everything up, then at her. How could she be so cold? Now, he was only angry at himself for being so stupid.

Cap put his hand firmly on Owen's shoulder. "You're going through a rough patch. I'm doing everything I can to try to help you through it."

Owen stepped back and looked at him. "It's a generous offer. I'll consider it."

* * *

Owen was kicking himself as he drove back to his condo. He hated letting Cap down, but Winnis Shipping was Cap's game, the way football had been at Penn. That was the tradition in their family for decades. The oldest son in each generation would be trained to take over Winnis Shipping. As soon as Cap had graduated with his Wharton MBA, he was named assistant vice president of the company.

Not surprisingly, he quickly worked his way up, making vice president by the time he was thirty and executive vice president—the number two man under their father, George Winnis III—a few years later. When Dad died suddenly three years ago, Cap stepped into the CEO role.

Meanwhile, over the years, Owen had tried to carve out his own area of expertise—being a professional slacker, as their mother would say. Going wherever he wanted around the world, writing what he really thought. And before the bombing, he was getting pretty good at it.

Now I have no clue what I'm going to do.

He did know one thing. He was not going to be the lame family ne'er-do-well on the dole. The first step toward figuring out what he wanted to do was to get back in the saddle.

Get real, Winnis, he could hear his high school buddy Donny saying. *How are you gonna dodge bullets and run from guerrillas with your gimpy leg? You're through as an international reporter.*

Owen pulled his Porsche into the entry drive of his condo building. The valet, Al, always looked suspiciously happy to see the little red car. Al opened the door for him, and Owen pulled himself out of the bucket seat, grunting as a splinter of pain shot through his shin.

"You got it there, Mr. Winnis?" Al asked.

"I think so." He handed Al a tip.

As soon as he entered his unit, he went to his office and turned on the computer.

He knew he was too weak to travel abroad right then, but how about pitching an investigative article on a scandal right here in Philadelphia? Surely *Time* or one of his other regular clients would publish something about political corruption or human rights violations at home. He knew he just needed to think of a good story to pitch.

There was the recent case involving the Temple student who appeared to be Arab or Middle Eastern, who was searched and illegally detained for over a month. The kid turned out to be exactly what he said he was—a doctoral student from Pittsburgh doing his thesis on Afghanistan. His mother was a Jewish woman from Israel, his father a Muslim from Syria, and he was born in the States, a U.S. citizen. How about "Stranger in My Own Home" as a title?

* * *

Hours later, he examined the computer screen. He had come up with six feature concepts he could pitch to a number of editors. He was in the zone and it felt good.

He looked at his watch. Nine forty-five. He needed to get something to eat.

First, something Cap said had been gnawing at him all evening. *This has to do with that woman.*

He went into his bedroom. The little gray felt box, a sad memorial to a dream, was still sitting on top of his dresser. He opened the box. The diamond was three carats, huge by most standards. When Owen bought it, however, it seemed like a paltry representation of his monumental love. He knew that no physical object could ever come close to representing how he felt at the time. Now the ring looked dull and ordinary, like a piece of costume jewelry.

What a joke, he thought as he tossed the box back behind his socks in the top drawer. *It will be a long time before I do that again.*

He had already come to terms with being alone once again. There was a great feeling of solace and independence in relying on oneself, as he had for so many years. You could grab a bag and be on the other side of the globe on twenty-four hours' notice.

He walked into the living room and decided he would check the headlines on the evening news, then go down to the restaurant on the ground floor.

"This is breaking news," anchor Lydia Parmont was saying the moment he turned on the TV. She wore a grim expression and her tone was grave and measured, as though giving an update on a military conflict.

"As I speak, fire engines have just arrived at the Winnis Shipping headquarters building on the Delaware River waterfront. Here's Glen Jamison at the scene."

"As you can see behind me," Jamison said, "the Winnis Building is engulfed in flames." The camera panned to the blazing building. "Authorities have not given a statement as to the cause, but there are reports from witnesses that there was an explosion on the top floor."

Owen was awestruck. Huge tongues of flames shot out of every window in the old brick edifice, and the top floor already looked gutted. Several streams of water from fire hoses poured onto the building to no discernible effect.

"Flaming debris from the blast has ignited one of Winnis's nearby oil tanks too," the reporter continued.

The camera panned over to show the flames reaching ten stories into the air. Then it continued panning, showing a sea of fuel tanks as yet untouched by the fire.

"I assume the first order of business is trying to make sure no other tanks catch fire."

Owen grabbed his crutch. *Cap will need some help getting this situation under control. Got to get down to the site as quickly as possible.*

As he went to the door, Lydia Parmont said, "One person close to the mayor's office has said they suspect this was a terrorist attack—"

Cap had reminded him, Winnis was a frequent terrorist target around the globe.

Now it's on our own shores.

* * *

The moment he drove out onto Columbus Boulevard, Owen could see the flames.

Greenwich Avenue, the short road leading to the Winnis Building, was blocked by police vehicles with flashing lights. They had set up a perimeter along Columbus Boulevard.

Owen jammed the Porsche into a spot at the nearest corner. As he got out, he could feel the explosive heat pounding at the side of his face. Close-up, the burning building did not seem any more real than on TV. He felt as though he were trapped in the worst kind of nightmare, the kind you can't awake from.

People had placed lawn chairs on the street opposite the police barriers and were gazing, awestruck, as if watching the Super Bowl halftime show.

The crowd grew thicker as he approached the burning building. Press crews stood nearby. The gusts of hot wind grew stronger. Through the smoke, he could make out the outlines of the one car in the Winnis parking lot. His stomach dropped. He hoped it wasn't Cap's Jag, but it was too badly burned to tell the make.

The crowd standing along the yellow tape parted to allow him to pass.

Amazing what a crutch and a scary look on your face can accomplish, he thought.

Behind the burning building, at the oil-tank fire, three red and white trucks marked "Chemical Control Unit" pumped foam onto the surrounding tanks.

Owen limped up to a patrolman standing next to a yellow police barricade, directing emergency vehicles. In an officious voice, the policeman said, "Not letting anyone through, sir."

Owen showed him his driver's license.

The patrolman conferred with someone over his walkie-talkie, then stepped aside. He pointed toward what looked like a large RV parked about thirty yards away. "Go to the incident command center over there."

Owen passed several firefighters in uniform rushing out of the command vehicle. With some difficulty, he pulled himself up the stairs. It was crammed with at least a dozen men, some in uniforms and others in street clothes, surrounded by walls of monitors and equipment with flashing lights. He looked around intently for a glimpse of his brother.

He recognized Police Commissioner Richard James, wearing a headset and standing in front of a monitor. Next to him was a Fire Department officer and several police officers.

"Hello, Owen," Commissioner James said loudly over the general din. "Very sorry for you and the Winnis family."

Owen blinked and nodded.

"Will Cap be coming?"

Owen looked around. "He's not here?"

"Haven't seen him."

A man vaguely recognizable as the fire commissioner shuffled over to them. The name Derek Evans came to mind.

"We have to make a preliminary statement to the press," Evans said to James.

"All we can say is that there are no known fatalities as yet," James said. "And we know it was a bomb. The arson team confirmed a C-4 device placed at the company's vault."

"Shouldn't we state the obvious?" Evans asked.

"That it's too soon to tell anything?" There was a sarcastic edge to James's answer.

"That it's terrorism." It sounded like a statement of fact.

"What, are you crazy? That could be inflammatory. Could be a burglary. And nobody has claimed responsibility."

"We could definitely say that it looks like a terrorist bombing—C-4 and all. That much is true."

"Let's say it could be a terrorist attack, among other possible causes."

Evans shrugged. "OK."

A fireman with a sergeant's hat rushed into the command center, his face covered with dark soot. He came over to Commissioner Evans. "They found a body."

"Where?"

"Top floor. About twenty yards away from the blast site. Partially dismembered by the blast."

Evans turned to Owen. "Was there a night watchman or security guard on the premises?"

"I don't know. Cap would know."

"Think you could reach him?"

Owen autodialed Cap's cell number. It went right to voice mail. Cap always left his cell phone on, even in the middle of the night. Owen again got the sick feeling in the pit of his stomach. He left a message anyway: "Cap, give me a call as soon as you get this."

Another fireman came into the command center and spoke quietly to the two commissioners. He turned and approached Owen.

Owen knew what he was about to hear.

Shadows

Shadows lie to live,
tell us we're taller, thinner,
flat as the earth was once
we thought; stalk us when
our backs are turned,

but the bright interrogator
must some of this blame share—

its radiant arrogance assigns
pools in deserts, floats false
diamonds on the sea, refracts
retinal images upside down—

poised between liars, we are
dazzled into believing these
beguiling truths, these inflated
casts of ourselves, of others;

powered by our breath, they
contrive with the sun to feign
friends by our side, leaving us
always to remember:

Shadows lie to live.

Broke

Somewhere in Buenos Aires there was a long and narrow passageway leading from a sunny patio to a heavy metal front door with several bolts and locks on it. The walls of the corridor were whitewashed many years ago and showed their age with thin angular cracks, at times large enough to reveal the bricks beneath the paint. There was an old moped near the door, a case of mineral water and various plants. A dozen of oranges lay carelessly thrown upon the patio floor made of tiny black and white ceramic tiles.

At a white plastic table in the center of the patio sat an apparently young man, drifting away in a reverie. On a table in front of him there was a notebook with a half-filled page of scribbles in black ink that looked like neat rows of tiny black ants. At least that is how it appeared to the voyeur hidden above, watching from the second floor window. Beside the notebook there was an ashtray, a pack of Lucky Strikes, a half-finished cup of coffee and a small prism. It was that last object that captivated the presumed writer. It could be seen from above that he was holding in his fingers an extinguished filter, topped with a tall head of ash.

The witness swears that she could see through the eyes of the man, and that she saw a trickle of tiny black ants streaming off the page in front of him, winding over the resting hand holding the butt of the long extinguished cigarette. Patiently, the exodus of words proceeded ahead in its insect-like composition, circumventing the unattended ashtray and the half-filled cup of coffee. Having crossed the span of the patio table, the procession entered through the prism, into the world of broken shades of perspectives.

* * *

The thin thread of his thoughts descended solemnly off the tabletop and down its leg, onto the patio floor that was a discontinuous chessboard. There, the single-minded stream of ants continued its laborious journey beneath the giant orange orbs carelessly left behind by runaway gods. It traversed the seemingly endless hallway, acutely aware that it existed at the edge of time and all the while sensing the minute subterranean tremors that underline the world and cause the cracks in the whitewashed walls.

Over time, the cordon of words reached the bolted door and scaled it with determination only insects are capable of. In this way the wandering mind arrived at the keyhole and labored through the rusted mechanism of the lock emerging into an illuminated world outside. It was a world bathed in unusually bright sunlight, a world of ever-forking streets that seem to expand continually in all directions, with new alleys angling away, as if the city unfolded itself as one passed through it.

* * *

In the grand scheme of things, inconsequential is the fate of any singular ant that may fall out of step and end its brief and illogical existence at a moment's notice. No sooner does the tiny black body stumble stiff-dead and it is consumed by those following it. The little things do not comprehend individually. They take no note of their own fate nor the terrain of the brightly lit cobble-stone labyrinth of the City. They navigate by purpose alone; without knowledge or conscience they go on, one little step after another.

The procession continues its momentum indefinitely and independently of the wandering mind out of which it was born. A mind confined beyond the bolted door of the patio with whitewashed walls, chessboard floors and scores of randomly placed oranges beneath which, minute vibrations and tremors murmur. A tectonic rift is developing beneath us - that of ages trembling ever so slightly apart, unnoticed by our shortsighted history.

It is the humming of the unsettling change that marks our age and appears upon the walls of the City in form of tiny cracks. If seen from a distant perspective, as if from a window in the sky, the thin thread of tiny ant-like words marching off the page, forms a definite and expanding fracture in the sunbathed fabric of rooftops, terraces, patios, alleys and checkered corridors. Corridors, just like the one where the apparently young man contemplates the secrets of the prism and the inevitable consequences that have shaped his life.

* * *

The witness observing from the second story window asserts that the world of the man below was not broken up by the prism that offered his mind a refuge. In her view it was the death of his second child, not so long ago, and the ongoing irrevocably failed marriage that drove him to the brink of paralysis. It was the looming bankruptcy of his soul at the price of survival and various other addictions of the self-mutilating economic machine that were the cause of his resignation. He retained a lot of anger, doubt and guilt, not to mention the credit card debts and anti-depressants. Above all, according to the witness, he was certain that everything that has happened to him happened as planned, with absolute disregard of his will.

To support this, the witness submitted a note that allegedly came from the notebook of the young man in question. It reads: "We go on like ants, persistently trudging ahead with the undeniable sense that all the pieces have been pre-arranged, so that they may fit the mind that conceived them. In time, the unbearable becomes bearable, even though the laws of this ancient game escape us. Who, is watched by whom, when all we really do is watch ourselves through others? What do we see then, when the fear sets in, and we realize that all this has been prepared just for us, and that we alone, in the heart of the loneliest of Cities, are the witnesses of our own undoing."

My Peace

"Hey, Johnny." It was my father, the best man I know. The wisest man, too. Guys at work call him *Buddha* for his bald little head and this little smile that says he knows something that no one else knows. I'm not wise like him and I hardly ever smile, 'cause it feels like something slimy's crawling across my face when I do, 'cause I'm thirteen and weird in a teenage sort of way—too skinny and tall, with a shaky voice and a dumb overbite, and the girls laugh at me, and there's rich poser kids and a moron who pushes me in the hall. Dad always listens nice and quiet when I complain, then he snaps the top off a beer can and says, "SNAFU, Johnny. Situation normal—dot dot dot."

No cursing for Dad.

He's a wise man, a wizard. No matter what happens—more yelling by mom, more crap from his boss—he takes it in stride, with a little Buddha smile like he's millions of miles away and at peace with the world.

I was in the doorway of The Sanctuary, and he waved me over to the worktable. "Did you ever wonder what true peace is like, son?"

I gave him that slimy grin to make him happy, but I couldn't look straight into his eyes—they're too bright and intense, full of super cosmic intelligence or something. Dad doesn't mind. He never tells me, Look me in the eye! like a teacher I know. So he just said, "Let's talk, John," with a friendly voice and a twinkly smile like the dads in the movies, those old black and whites. He's my own movie dad. And he knows real life, not the bookworm crap they feed you in school. I smiled full out. Only my dad makes my smile feel good.

The Sanctuary is our garage, and Dad loves it. He's got a little fridge full of beers for him and soda for me that he keeps locked, he keeps everything locked 'cause he's such a great dad—first–aid, safe driving, all that. He's got a bench and a barbell—he's small, but you can see how pumped he is in the arms and chest when he wears a tee shirt— and he's got a work table where he fixes broken lamps and stuff while listening to football or sports talk or politics. Once we rented *Hunchback Of Notre Dame*, the black–and–white one, and when we went to the garage to get away from the drama in the house he said "Sanctuary!" in The Hunchback's weird voice. It's been The Sanctuary ever since.

"Thirteen's a special age, Johnny. You're becoming a man."

I felt my smile go slimy 'cause I knew he was lying.

"Do you know what happens when a Jewish boy turns thirteen? It's a rite of passage, and they call him a man. Did you know that?"

"It's called a bar something." The only Jewish person I knew was my math teacher, and he made me feel dumb with this look on his face that was supposed to be friendly, but really he was laughing at you.

"But John," he said, pointing at his head, "they don't know." He winked at me like he had a great secret to tell from ancient times or the edge of space. Then he put his hand under my chin and lifted it up so that I had to look him in the eyes. His smile got bigger, and I smiled back just like him. "Do you ever wonder about absolute peace?" he said. It sounded like church talk, except we never go. "Do you ever wonder about absolute quiet?" I didn't understand, but his smile was so nice that I kept looking at him. "You've heard the expression *peace and quiet*, right, son?"

I nodded. Dad has this way of pulling me along when we talk. He absolutely should have been a teacher. He's ten times smarter than the real teachers.

"Remember how peaceful it was in the woods last summer?"

I nodded. Last summer we went camping, just us two, and sat by the river just listening to the water for hours, not talking at all. I'm not exaggerating. We did not talk for hours.

"You can have that same kind of peace right here in the city. You can have the quiet that brings the peace."

He reached into his pocket for his big key ring that had about fifteen keys and found the one that unlocked the drawer beneath the worktable. I thought maybe he was hiding a bottle of Jack Daniels in there and would let me have a sip, a rite of passage like a Jewish kid having wine at his bar thing. Or maybe he'd initiate me into smoking grass with his medical marijuana, or maybe he had some Buddhist prayer beads or something.

"Son," he said. "Put your hand out, palm up. And close your eyes." I did what he said. "Now feel that, son."

It felt so good, so cool in my hand. So heavy and smooth. Dad closed my hand around the grip, which had a nice pebbly feel, and slipped my finger through the trigger guard and set it on the trigger. "You can open 'em now."

He was holding my hand in both of his hands with the barrel of the gun pointed at the floor. The gun wasn't loaded, but he told me in a very serious way to never point a gun at a living person even if you're sure it's unloaded.

"Now Johnny," he said. "Did you ever feel total command? Did you ever have the feeling of making the entire world stand still, like it's at your command?"

It was a silly question, so I ignored it. But like I said, he should've been a teacher, because he's always a step ahead of my thinking, always pulling me along until I realize that I know stuff that I didn't know that I knew 'til he shows me.

"John, think. Did you ever feel like you're—"—he stopped and gave me this epic wise man look that went deep inside of me, and lowered his voice like a movie trailer guy—"master of the universe?"

"Yeah!" I said. My favorite game.

"And that part where you finally corner Dreyghon, and he puts down his weapon and gets on his knees and begs you not to kill him? And you put your gun right to his head and just ... listen?"

"Yeah," I said.

"You know that feeling you get? Of absolute peace?"

"Yeah," I said. I played that part over and over just to see Dreyghon shut his big fat ugly fish face for once.

Dad mussed up my hair. It was funny that he had to reach up to do it.

"Imagination is the key to finding peace, to escaping the aggravation of the world. Did you know they did studies that if you imagine a thing, you feel the thing? And the thing becomes real in your mind, the way your neurons fire and everything?" I nodded, more with excitement than understanding. "They've done studies on these Buddhist swamis that astral project—you know, leave their bodies, transport themselves across a river or something. They put electrodes on their brains, and you can see their bodies still sitting there, but their brain waves are going crazy, like they're really flying. Or they make themselves feel fire or ice even if there isn't any. Like hypnotism, sort of. See what I mean?"

"Yeah," I said.

"Great! So that's what we're doing. Now listen, Johnny. I want you to picture someone who chaps your hide, like that smart ass math teacher, or some stuck up chick, or that SOB bully. Okay?"

We have a dart board against a wall in The Sanctuary. Dad pulled a picture of a black shadow of a human head from the gun drawer, a silhouette, and pinned it to the dart board. "Alright now. Who's your target?"

I smiled up at him like I couldn't believe I could do this. He read my mind and nodded that I could, and I started thinking of people, but there were so many to choose from that I couldn't decide.

"Well," he said, `cause he really can read my mind, "there was that big mouth animal rights activist who stuck that flyer in our face when we were trying to enjoy our ribs in peace." Yeah, she was a jerk. "Or those gun control nuts who go on TV every time some fool goes off and gives us all a bad name. You'll settle on someone. Just meditate on it."

So I closed my eyes with the gun in both hands and the barrel pointed at the floor with Dad's hand on my hands, and meditated with the biggest smile ever. Then I opened my eyes and lifted the gun to the dart board.

"Got someone in mind? Excellent. Now I want you to imagine them chapping your hide with their stupid words, like that math teacher or those rich snots, or that punk shoving you in the hall. It's all good."

"I got it," I said.

"Alright," he said. "Now just lift the piece up nice and steady and press it to their forehead."

I pressed the gun to the math teacher's head.

"Now listen," Dad said.

I listened.

"What do you hear?"

"Nothing," I answered. "He like, totally stopped talking."

"Darn right," said Dad.

"It's just quiet," I said.

He smiled as if I was super bright.

He took the gun from me and locked it in the gun drawer.

I don't have the key, and Dad won't get me my own piece until I'm eighteen— but I visit The Sanctuary with Dad whenever someone chaps me, and I find my peace there.

Earth to Earth

Told you to leave me alone. Look the other way. Don't pull me out of the fire, don't get me off the hook, don't rescue this here lamb from the wolves. Once my flesh has been burned away, I will have an idea of why I should avoid the fire next time. Once I opened my mouth to try and catch that shiny, moving object and it has lodged itself in my upper jaw, the other end of the hook protruding through my left eye, I shall avoid those spawning rivers. Once I have lain with the rascal wolf and he has eaten my heart I shall be alert to the danger of the hunter. Look the other way. Why else did I commence this blood journey but to experience the joy of pain, the enslavement of lust and the overcoming of fear. You will be found pressed between the pages of moldy ancient tomes. Parchment to parchment.

Laughing All the Way to the Bank is
No Laughing Matter

It started with the small bits. They were the first to be falling off. Odd stories were whispered and then hushed. The stories were later reported and then much later reenacted on late night comedy shows. But then it got personal, closer to home.

Like the time the lady in front of you at the grocery store, gave her gold card to the cashier and in the process her pinky fell. She screamed, you screamed and then everyone else screamed as her pinky finger was swept, kicked and stepped on. You ran home: "I saw it! It happens just like on YouTube!"

"What happened?" they asked. So you told them how the poor lady's dried up and flaky pinky plopped off like a scab that had been drying up for some time.

The incidents became normal, an everyday occurrence. People stopped screaming.

An ear here. A big toe there.

The most important gossip was finding out who was the best and cheapest surgeon. Friends would go in together for the special "Two for the Price of One!"

Later larger things began falling and again these would be reenacted on comedy shows and searched out on YouTube. These soon also became the norm.

The tabloids of course loved to plaster the stars' pictures. Pictures magnified to the tenth degree of their newly reattached fingers or ears. Nobody was impressed. They had money, didn't they? They had access to the best plastic surgeons, right? But still, beneath the resentment and hostility, the realization sank in. It happened, even to them, the stars.

Word got out about the poor doctors and those not yet out of med school, overwhelmed by public demand, making horrifying blunders. Some developed gangrene or had their items sewn on backwards looking like bloody Frankenstein's monsters. This, of course was shown, horrifyingly on the news channels and hilariously on the comedy shows.

It happened so fast and so often that everyone either had a horrifying story or a hilarious one to tell which was conveniently taped or photographed. Since it all happened so fast and on a worldwide scale, every Sunday night millions of families around the globe were glued to the televisions to watch, "World's Global Funniest Falling Apart Bloopers."

These shows were so popular, so hilarious, that they ran into one series after another, with DVD releases and constant reruns.

All eyes were on the $10,000 prize which was available to anyone, because everyone was falling apart. How the world roared and cried and laughed itself silly over the footage: Talks of world peace were in motion. Enemies in underdeveloped countries sat side by side watching the local television. Religious hatred was set aside, compassion and hilarity held hands.

Endless predictable scenarios brought us to tears of laughter. Scenarios of the bride and groom, whose eyes grew big and wide, looking into the audience for solace, as the groom held the bride's ring finger in his hand with the officiating priest breaking into giggles, and then the audience and finally the poor newly wedded, all joining in the shocked laughter.

The groom would hold the ring finger in the air dripping with blood and yell with pride or mumble in shock, "Till death do us apart!" or "I guess it's coming nearer than we thought."

Or how the bride would throw her bouquet and the ladies would cluster around her with wide smiles only to end up screaming in horror and fleeing the scene as the one lucky lady received both the bouquet and the bride's hand.

Hidden cameras were set up in places we never thought to look. All captured on tape for our enjoyment.

They were set up in the kitchens, filming the chefs slaving away in the heat. If you looked carefully as the camera zoomed in, a finger, or worse yet an ear would plop into the soup or cake. Then the hilarious desperate scramble would ensue as they tried to clean the mess up. The poor horrified cook stood looking like a hunted rabbit as another worker whisked the plate away into the hands of a confused waiter who then ran out to present the food to the waiting patrons in the restaurant.

They were placed in locker rooms, in cafeterias, at gas stations, in bathrooms, everywhere. And everywhere the people that they filmed had the same curious expression, the "What is this?" and the same horrified wide-eyed gasping look that left us all clutching our sides.

Like the teenager new on the job at the Nike shoe store in the mall. Obviously nervous, yet so gentlemanly as he helped the woman put on her requested shoe and then the poor kid rattling the shoes, crawling on the floors searching for the woman's big toe .

Or the sweet pretty girl humming and singing to herself in the mirror, unaware of the camera filming nearby, running her fingers through her hair, checking herself out, until inevitably the wide-eyed confused, "What is this?" came over her face as she used both hands to undo the tangle that developed in her long tresses to pull finally, through the knots and twists, her ear.

Or the professor so serious in his monologue before the sleeping audience, but then suddenly the whole house awake and laughing as he stood in confusion as his left arm plopped off, landing with a big thud.

The cameras caught scientists in their labs giggling as they developed devices that were for practical uses and they were ever so careful, ever so conscious to avoid the falling body parts.

They even caught that famous plastic surgeon from California. The "patients" came into his office with serious faces, asking him if he really did know what he was doing, if he really did go to a reputable university and not a diploma mill cranking out fake PhDs. The doctor alarmed would straighten up and say, "Yes, look at my diplomas here and over there. Ask my clients. Yes, of course I know what I'm doing."

Yet, still they continued. They gathered closer to him and that tiny secret camera pinned to one of the "patients" blouse would zoom in on the doctor's face as she asked "Don't you ever think you need a break, or a vacation, or feel overwhelmed at all by the pressures of the job?"

The doctor would say adamantly over and over, "No I don't need a vacation! I am not overwhelmed...not even a little bit." We all watched his anger boil inside of him, turn his face a bright pink then red as he demanded, "What is this all about?"

They wouldn't answer. "Are you sure you don't feel overwhelmed by the present responsibilities of your job?"

"No, no!" he cried and then they all politely nodded and made room for the one patient that had been standing behind . The patient held out his hand as they asked, "Then how do you explain this?"

The doctor gasped staring at this patient's hand with his four fingers naturally curved downward, and the one thumb that was sewn on the wrong way, poking backwards straight up into the air. He broke out into laughter, shaking his head in shock and in embarrassment. And they all joined him, laughing and teasing him, "Are you sure? Are you sure you're not under any pressure?"

Or even the host himself, as he stood on national television about to introduce the next clip. He stumbled and stammered as his ear fell off onto his shoulder and then bounced into his suit's front breast pocket, leaving an obvious bulge. The audience, at first stunned, finally roared as he looked around in confusion asking everybody, "What? What is it?" Because he genuinely, truly did not know what had just happened.

Nobody was immune and we all accepted this with grace, with humor, and with dignity.

Of course, nobody laughed when heads started to fall off. The world turned to sorrow. Scientists screamed and cursed at their gadgets as they bobbed up and down, reaching for their heads. Their giggles turning into great sobs, like water running from the tap.

Taxidermy

James River State Park Visitor's Center,
Summer 2013

We start out happy.
My 8-month-old finds his needs filled
and just smiles and laughs
like a baby fool drunk
on love.
The innocence is in him
fueling his sounds,
his full eyes.

Then we grow.
We find tiny injustices
and wane a bit.
It's the way looking a stuffed black bear
in the eyes can give you nightmares.
You're not allowed to touch
an animal long dead
but you want to.
Posed in death to stand tall.
As tall as any man would fear.
But I'm sorry bear,
you'll not get
the best of me.

My 5 year old has his needs filled
and wants more.

Understanding begins to fill his eyes.
He sees the bear
and refuses to linger.
Refuses to look that bear solid
in the eye.
He poses in front of the deer.
Nothing we need to fear
in her subtle pose.

Sweetness cannot follow fear
unless you let it.
We settle into patterns
like a circle.
Find the black bear inside us,
and the doe
in our hearts.

The Remains of Her Son

Rain. Falling on the inn's red-tiled roof that slants sharply over the veranda. Sluicing over the low-hanging edge of the roof, falling and glittering in a white-water curtain. The veranda, deep and always shadowy even on a sunny day, surrounds the inn and shields the first-floor rooms from the pelting rain. Bundled up in my raincoat, I walk quick-stepped onto the veranda and set down the two bags of groceries and household supplies on the cement floor, next to the entrance door.

The roadside inn where I live and work is old in the deep south of the Mekong Delta. During the war this was the IV Corps that had seen many savage fights. Though the battle carnage might have long been forgotten, some places are not. They are haunted.

The owner and his wife of the second generation are in their late sixties. The old woman runs the inn, mainly cooking meals for the guests, and I would drive to Ông Đốc town twenty kilometers south to pick up customers when they arrive by land on buses or by waterways on boats and barges. Most of them come to visit the Lower U Minh National Reserve, a good twenty kilometers north of the inn. I seldom see the old man. He is mostly holed up in their room. Sometimes when its door isn't locked, you might see him wander about like a specter. The man is amnesiac and cuckoo.

It's forenoon now. It rained when I went into town. Rain hasn't let up. Water started rising on the roads on my way back from the town. On a rainy day like this, Mrs. Rossi stays home. She came to this region to search for the remains of her son, a lieutenant who went missing-in-action during the Vietnam War.

I recommended a man, a war veteran, whom Mrs. Rossi eventually hired to help her search for the bones of her son. Back then, within a year after the war, people here were familiar with the sight of the poor citizens who traveled to this land looking for their lost husbands, sons, relatives. Sometimes you would see soldiers but they didn't stay at the inn. They would camp in the woodland with their trucks and it would be a week or even longer before they left. There were many soldiers coming to this region. Came in organized groups called Remains-Gathering Crew. During the war thousands of them were stationed in this region, always deep in the swamp forest. Many died. Most of them died from bombing and shelling and ground assaults. Deaths were common back then. And death discriminates no one. In that forbidden swamp forest you had flesh and bones of the soldiers on both sides and the flesh and bones of Americans. All lay under the peat soil.

We also have new guests who arrived at the inn three days ago. A couple from Ireland. They drove down long-distance from Hồ Chí Minh City. The husband is some sort of a journalist. Since their arrival he has gone around the U Minh region always with a camera, a backpack, and a palm-sized voice recorder. The wife, in her late thirties, made friends easily with us. When she first heard of the purpose of Mrs. Rossi's visit, she said to her, "Jasus, ye break my heart."

The door opens with the familiar scratching noise the bottom-edge wire mesh makes against the cement floor. Since I came, I have sealed each door's bottom edge with a wire mesh to keep out bugs and rodents and even snakes especially during floods. Chi Lan stands in the doorway, holding a mug in her hand.

"*Chú*," she says, "give me a grocery bag." Her voice is soft with a lilt in 'chú.' Uncle.

She came to the inn with her American mother, Mrs. Rossi, who adopted her in 1974 when she was five years old. She's nineteen now.

I put the bag in the crook of her arm. "Where's everyone?"

"My Mom's in the back with Maggie," she says. "Washing clothes. Alan went off somewhere in their car."

I notice steam rising from her mug. "What're you drinking?"

"Café *phin*. I made it myself."

"Black?"

"No. With condensed milk. I can't drink it black like you."

"I've got you into drinking Vietnamese slow-drip café now, huh?" I get out of my raincoat and hang it on a wall hook several of which I have put up on the veranda walls, front and back, for guests to hang up their raincoats before they enter the inn.

She steps back for me to come in. Barefooted, her toenails look rosy, freshly polished.

"We'll be even when I get you to quit smoking," she says.

I smile at her gentle tone. I have indeed thought of cutting back on smoking. It is cool inside the house. Her black T-shirt and black hair blend with the dimness, and her white shorts are the only bright color as the whitewashed walls. My sandals squeak, leaving a wet trail behind me on the gray cement floor. Clean looking as the old woman of the inn demands it. At the end of the big room is a pantry that has a refrigerator. Chi Lan sets her mug on a shelf and puts groceries into the refrigerator. Suddenly she stops and holds up a paper-wrapped baguette.

"*Bánh mì!*" she sounds as if she's just found gold.

"Yeah," I say. "I bought plenty of them for lunch. Hope you and everyone'd like it."

"I love it. What do we have in them?" She takes off the rubber band, opens the wrapper and peeks inside the baguette. The fillings seem to please her as she sniffs at the pork bellies and liver pâté garnished with cilantro, chili peppers, cucumber slices, and pickled carrots. "I've tried to make these at home," she says, wrapping up the baguette and ties it with the rubber band, "and they never came out like this—the smell, the taste."

"Because most of the fillings are homemade. The pork bellies in particular. They made the bread themselves too. Didn't you know that?"

"And because I'm an amateur cook." She taps her cheek with the wrapped baguette, picks up her mug and sips. "Are you a good cook, chú?"

"I can manage on my own." I walk to the cupboard that stands by the door into the kitchen. "Alan asked me about a snake dish the other day. I told him before he and his wife leave, I'd cook a snake dish for everyone."

"Oh my." She closes the refrigerator. "Did you tell him you used to catch snakes with your father? Did you? And about the snake gallbladder?"

"No. I've never told anyone that. Except you." I set down the supplies bag, squatting on my heels, and inspect the four legs of the cupboard, each leg shod with a tin cup half filled with vinegar. In one cup floats a mass of dead black ants.

The air stirs faintly as she kneels beside me. "Must be the sugar jar in the cupboard that attracted them. Look at them." She bends closer, sweeping back her hair over her ear. "That looks like a moat around a fortress—the water and the cups. Is this your idea, chú?"

"Yeah."

"You're a good custodian with a whole lot of good ideas."

"It's not water in those tin cups. It's vinegar."

She looks again. "What's the difference?"

"Ants might survive in water and they'll crawl up those legs into the cupboard."

"I didn't know vinegar kills them." She turns to face me, her eyes gently holding my gaze. "My Mom appreciated having that clothing trunk in our room to store our clothes. I didn't know why it's lined with tin till you told us. Otherwise our old suitcases if we'd used them would've crawled with moths and cockroaches."

"I'm going to replace the vinegar in those cups." I take out a bottle of vinegar in the bag. "When I lift a leg up, can you remove the cup under the leg for me?"

"Go ahead, chú."

She remains on her knees, head bent, as I plant my feet and slowly raise a corner of the cupboard. I glance down as she slides the cup out, and through the open top of her T-shirt I can see that she's braless. I hold my breath, set the cupboard back down. She tilts her face up at me.

"What now? Should I empty the cup—and the ants?"

"Yeah."

Each time I heave the cupboard, despite my knowing what I will see when I drop my gaze at her, I still look down through the crescent opening below her clavicles, holding my gaze at the milky white of her skin, the fullness of her bosom, and what comes back to my mind is a child's innocent eyes and a man's disturbed thoughts.

* * *

On the rear veranda Mrs. Rossi and Maggie, the Irish woman, are scrubbing clothes in a round rubber tub. The woman innkeeper normally does this chore. Though old, she can still scrub and wring garments with her small hands. At times she would tread on them the old-fashioned way while her hands hoist the legs of her pantaloons.

"Giang," Mrs. Rossi calls to me, "you're back already."

Maggie, her face wet, raises her voice with a toss of her head, "Made it back in one piece in this bloody weather, didn't ye?"

"Roads are flooded now," I say to them. "Where's your husband, Maggie?"

"Went to meet his local guide and then off to the jungle." She meant the U Minh forest. "I said go aisy on a day like this. He's beyant control. Wouldn't you say, Katherine?"

Mrs. Rossi shrugs. I step closer and look down at her lower legs. Above her ankles are crowds of deep purple marks like she has been hit with a buckshot.

"Leech bites?" I ask her, pointing at them.

"How d'you know by just looking?" Mrs. Rossi looks at her ankles and up at me.

"I've got scars on my legs from them." I pull up my trousers legs. The women and Chi Lan stare at the pea-sized scars on my shins, my calves.

Her face scrunched up, Chi Lan shakes her head. "You've got them during the war, chú?"

"From years in the jungles."

Mrs. Rossi drops a wrung-out sock into an empty basket next to the tub. "Every night when I take off my socks, they're bloodstained from those suckers. The first few days in the forest I was near tears from putting up with them. Mr. Lung, he seemed unperturbed by leeches and bugs. You know how he got rid of those leeches for me?"

"With his cigarettes?" I say. "Make them drop away?"

"That or I just pulled them off my legs."

"That's why you've got scars like these." I sit down on my heels, put my fingertip on her calf and slide a finger under the fingertip. "Do like this. Slide your fingernail under the sucker's mouth. It'll break off. Won't leave any scar mark on you I guarantee."

"What else is better than that?"

"I'll get you the chopped tobacco. All you have to do is soak them in water. Then soak your socks in the tobacco water and then dry them socks before you wear them. Leeches won't bother you again."

"What do you think of that? Does it really work?"

Grinning, I nod. "Or you can cut a leech in half."

Mrs. Rossi leans back slowly looking at me and smiles. "I've heard if you do that, it'll regenerate itself. True?"

"No, ma'am. And I'm glad Mother Nature is fair to us that way."

Maggie laughs. "That'll do us all the good in the world, won't it?"

She rises with the tub in her arms and empties it over the edge of the veranda and fills the tub with rainwater sluicing like waterfall from the edge of the roof. I have seen her and Chi Lan washing themselves with rainwater, cleaning and scrubbing themselves until their faces glowed. Precious rainwater. When it rains I would fill jugs of rainwater for the old woman to wash and bathe the old man, for cooking and drinking, too. Once, while filling the jugs, I told Chi Lan that in the jungles we soldiers used to wait for rain so we could shower, and sometimes it was just a passing shower which stopped before we could get all the suds off our bodies. She laughed.

"Is she sleeping around this time?" Chi Lan looks back into the house for the old lady.

"She's feeding him," I say.

"You want me to fill the water jugs for her?" Chi Lan says.

"No." My hand touches my shirt pocket where the cigarette pack is. "We have all we need for now."

I catch her gaze at my gesture for a smoke. I leave my hand on my chest and in my mind I see the creamy white skin of her bosom. She squats down and begins scrubbing a mud stain off her mother's jeans in the tub.

Mrs. Rossi arches her back, drawing a deep breath. "I must say I admire the old lady for washing clothes like this. My back is already killing me."

Maggie is wringing her denim shirt until veins bulge on the backs of her hands. "That's why that oul' lady walks bowlegged." She shakes the shirt loudly. "Mother o' God give us a washer and a dryer. That's wan thing we need here."

I have told them to air-dry their clothes in the sun once a week, so the sun would kill any eggs that might have been deposited in their garments. Books they bring with them too. Shake them out once in a while. On the first day of their arrival I heard her scream upstairs. I saw a trail of black ants that led into their room and heard her say to Alan, her husband, "I won't touch that thing for the steam of their piss." So I went in and there I saw a dead scorpion under the dresser. I picked up the scorpion and told them I would get rid of the ants for them. "Oh you're a treasure," she said to me. "Please make them bloody eejit go 'way."

Now she hangs up her shirt on the cord strung across the veranda and clips it with a wooden clothes-peg. In her late thirties she is lean, small-bosomed, her sandy-blonde hair tied into a ponytail. Bony in the face that's freckled heavily under the eyes, clear blue eyes, she smiles a lot, the ear-to-ear smile that brings a smile to your face. She comes back to the tub for her cotton slacks. "You ever got caught with this sorta rain in the jungle while ye go about yeer business?" she asks Mrs. Rossi.

"Oh I've been in those downpours and the misting after the monsoon rains. It's miserable, Maggie."

"Tell me, love, how on earth can ye find anything in such a place? In that wilderness God doesn't plant a sign that says, Dig here! Ye know what I mean."

Skimming the suds off Chi Lan's forearm with her finger, Mrs. Rossi smiles softly. She hugs her knees, her pale blue eyes blink a few times as they rove from my face to Maggie's. "Mr. Lung has a method," she said, her voice trembling a little. "He's done this before. So we kinda divided up the area and went from one section to the next. We'd spot a mound of earth here and there and I was all excited to see any of them. He'd dig and dig, bless his old heart, 'cause he never stopped going till I begged him to take a breather. Then all he did is take a sip of water, have a smoke, and then he'd be back at it. Most of the times we found nothing. A few times we found bones, human bones, and God Almighty I'd feel myself shaking. And you know something? You can't tell one skull from another. They all look like they were cast from the same mold. But come to think of that. Those unclaimed bones, unidentified skulls must've belonged to some unknown soldiers and that's why somebody like me is still searching for them. Or they might've already given it up."

Listening to Mrs. Rossi, I couldn't help thinking the same thought. You can't tell those skulls apart. You can't tell a Vietnamese skull from an American skull.

Mrs. Rossi coughs a small cough and her white-haired head keeps shaking like she can't chase away something unpleasant in her head. "One time we found this Penicillin bottle among the bones. It's closed tight with a rubber cap. Mr. Lung opened it and there's nothing but a piece of paper inside. Well, he doesn't speak English like you, Giang, but after a lot of gesticulating and with much pidgin English, he got me to understand that it had to do with a soldier's identification. Things like name, combat unit, rank, birthplace and hometown. He said back when the Remains-Gathering Crew would arrive searching for the remains of their comrades, the bones they found with no Penicillin bottles would be brought back with those identified and buried in the National Military Cemetery. Except that the unidentified bones would be interred in the section for the remains of unknown Vietnamese soldiers."

Maggie frowns. "I thought the Americans must've bombed the bejesus outa the jungle. So what's left in there to find?"

I cut in. "You rebury the remains. Sometimes all you rebury are a few bones. The rest got blown away."

"And if ye find them," Maggie says, "how d'ye take them oul' bones back?"

"For mass recovery of bones?" I plug a cigarette in my mouth without lighting it. "They pack them in nylon bags and hang them on tree limbs. Keep them away from termites 'cause the Remains-Gathering Crew would stay in the forest for weeks. They'll bring all the bags of bones back to the cemetery when their stay is over."

Her lips puckered, Maggie screws her eyes at me. "Just a funny thought: Say ye stumble on a skull of an orangutan. Can ye tell? Or ye bag it up and bury it in your National Military Cemetery among the oul' souls of yeer soldiers?"

Mrs. Rossi tilts her head back and from that angle eyes Maggie with an inquisitive yet bemused look on her face. I take the cigarette from my lips. "The men of the Remains-Gathering Crew have a way of knowing about bones. They know how to tell a monkey skull from a human skull. A woman's skull from a man's skull . . ."

"Seriously?" Maggie chirps up.

"Yeah," I say, grinning. "They can tell. A woman's chin bone is smaller than a man's chin bone. The eye sockets are deeper. That sort of things."

"Ah, now," Maggie says, nodding. "Nurses, aren't they?"

"Soldiers. Women fighters."

Mrs. Rossi gently wipes bubbling foam off Chi Lan's cheek. "We did find a couple of skulls and Mr. Lung said they're women's skulls. I had the faintest idea why he said that, based on what logics is beyond me. But women soldiers?"

I told them the women's skulls must have belonged to a vanguard unit of women fighters who took risks to spearhead the enemy's territories. That was their mission. All of them were women.

Maggie whistles. "All women, eh? Aw for Jaysus sake . . ."

Mrs. Rossi lets out a sigh. "Mr. Lung was respectful with the bones we found. You must see how careful he was with those bones when he came upon them…"

"He's a gravedigger and a undertaker around here," I say.

"I remember you telling me that," Mrs. Rossi says. "I admire him for his professionalism but more so for his personal feeling in the way he treated the dead people's bones. Before he dug he'd light a stick of incense. Then you just watch him stab and stab the ground with his shovel and sometimes it'd hit rocks and sparks'd fly and then he suddenly stopped and looked down and there lay a small bundle in the hole, just a nylon bunch tattered and gray and when he ran his hand over it the nylon fell apart. Like ashes. A skull cracked and chipped. Like broken china."

"What'd he do with them?" Maggie asks. "In the name of Jaysus, Mary and Holy St. Joseph!"

Mrs. Rossi's eyes turn pensive and her voice drops. "He'd rewrap the bones in a clean piece of nylon he brought with him and he'd shovel dirt over the pit and say a prayer."

I feel as if she's living her wish through Old Lung's acts to see her son's remains ever cared for by a stranger in a time and place unknown. Then Mrs. Rossi speaks again.

"After he reburied the bones and sometimes bones with a skull, Mr. Lung'd flatten the dirt and remove the incense stick. I asked him why he did that and he explained, well, sorta miming with the help of his infantile English, that'd wipe out any sign of a grave. God, why, I asked. So the bad people wouldn't come upon it, he said. That's as far as I could get to the truth of this whole befuddling thing."

She looks at me. Her wrinkled face, crimped lips hold in them a dogged patience. I tap the cigarette on my thumbnail. "Mr. Lung did the right thing," I say, resting myself on one knee. "There're bone crooks who go around digging up bones and sell them."

"Selling bones?" Mrs. Rossi's mouth falls agape.

"They're swindlers. Bone profiteers."

"Selling bones to whom?" Mrs. Rossi asks.

"To contractors who build the National Military Cemetery."

"I might be obtuse," Mrs. Rossi says. "Would you please explain *that?*"

"These bone crooks would go into the forests and dig for bones. The worst of them would follow the poor folks after they've recovered the bones of their relatives and outright rob them of the bones. Then these crooks would sell the bones to the contractors in the city. You see, ma'am, for each tomb the contractors build its cost is charged to the government, so the more tombs built the higher the profit. The contractors would divide up the bones they bought from the bone crooks, and instead of building one tomb for a dead soldier's bones they build two, three tombs and charge the government for those. For the unknown remains, they'll end up having several unknown markers for one dead soldier. But worse, ma'am, are those having been recovered by their relatives and later robbed by the bone crooks. So instead of being properly buried back home with a tomb and a headstone, a dead soldier will be buried in the National Military Cemetery as an unknown soldier with his bones in multiple tombs."

Mrs. Rossi nods, her pale blue eyes completely vacant as she looks at me. Maggie taps her forehead. "Aw Gawd I shure never heard of this meself."

"Me neither," Mrs. Rossi says. "Who could've thought of doing such inhuman thing?"

I gaze at her wrinkled face as she tosses her head back, fanning her face with her hand. *Why a Vietnamese adopted child?* Did it let her hold on to the memory of her lost son? I like Mrs. Rossi. A retired high school principal. A sweet old lady. I admire her determination to find her son's remains. More so, I admire her faith. Painful faith. Yet it never dies in her after twenty years.

Burn Dirt in the Name

At regular tea you
lower your last finger

to say, "There's no need for Poughkeepsie.
Have it removed."
Across from you I'm wondering
who that dark child is
and what it is he keeps
repeating : "Ethnowhat?

Ethnono! Ethnowhat?"

As he circles your chair
I notice that you don't
notice him as you say
something about "Burning
and razing the dirt...
Replacing the discarded

in the name of progress
and image of class..."

You argue it can be
done away with like a child
that got in the way, making up words
and darkened the space
that should be rightly given
to proper ceremony under the growing

sweep of civilization.

At regular tea
you right my last nerve
and I sway.

"Well, have the dark removed, for everyone's sake"

The Man on the Bridge

I'm beginning the third layer of my watercolor painting. This is the aquamarine layer, over a crimson red spread across yellow. The order doesn't matter; this is just the way it goes today. The sun is hot, so between layers I lie back on a bed of ivy and ruminate. Obsess perhaps, or so says Wally. Wally likes to stand above me, watch my blonde hair spread out like a forest of kelp in the sea. When I obsess, he says, my lenses move back and forth under my closed eyelids like the pendulums of grandfather clocks.

I'm painting the floodwaters gushing below the Third Avenue Bridge. My morning has burned away like so much kindling, even in this saturated place. The bridge is not crossable. Pounding waves erode the abutment, the piers no longer stable. I should have crossed much earlier, days before, but I lingered on this side too long.

I can see now a man breaking through the barriers set to stop traffic. He's forced the yellow girder aside, climbed through. He hauls a parcel from the other side, something lopsided and bumpy wrapped in a golden tarp. He's walking backwards, pulling the bundle by the plaited rope woven through grommets.

I drizzle water over the lower third of my painting, more on the left than the right. I want to blend the colors. An orange haze creeps up the paper. Little veins emerge, moving against gravity. They intersect with the aquamarine and form brief horizontal lines, a code of some sort. On my palette, I mix burnt sienna with copious amounts of water, then fill my size 8 blunt round brush. The paint has a will of its own. I roll the paint back and forth, tilting the paper from side to side, careful not to cross into the space I've left empty in the center. I consider filling the void with the absurd little man crossing the bridge. He's sheared the rope on jagged rocks that had washed onto the bridge when the creek crested. He struggles to hold his load together. Every knot he ties unravels.

Wally must be wondering by now where I've gone off to. My cell phone has been dead two days and my picnic basket contains only cellophane and onions. The floodwaters are dark with rage, cursing against the creek bank. Too thick with sludge to drink. Yesterday, I saw a cow floating by with a red bandana tied around her neck. Her big round eyes pleaded with me to free her from the current.

I have three sheets left on my watercolor block. This includes the painting in progress. My father tells me the best paper is cold pressed. Each year he sends me nine twenty-page blocks of 140 lb Arches. I tell him every year I will not be painting one-hundred-eighty pieces. He says I set limits before I begin and that has always been my problem. My father knows no limits.

There's an incessant prickle crawling down the right side of my back, reaching past my hip and crossing over my belly. Wally has warned me about daydreaming on ivy. The poison kind may appear innocent at times. Perhaps urushiol has invaded. The oil pervades, attaches without warning. I pull a blade from my bamboo brush-mat and scale the detritus of my contaminated flesh away. I notice the man on the bridge is losing his patience. He's begun tossing his belongings into the water.

It's still raining upcreek. Just eight miles away, a torrent of water falls. People continue to sump pump basements and drive through water too deep. Firefighters risk their lives to pull men, women and children—sometimes dogs—from waters intentionally violated. The death count climbs. Houses wash away. Water rises at the drycleaners, causing dirty laundry to fill the streets.

I admire the effect of burnt sienna on the page. Cast iron gray clouds obscure the sun, making the drying process tedious. The distance across is growing larger for the man on the bridge. He's shed all the wares he can tolerate and pulled what's left of his rope taut. Already tainted, I lie back on the ivy and rest.

I wake to a bilious rumbling, the noise, the earthy smell, moving layers of soil seeping out from under the place where I'd slept, spilling into the creek. I reach for my brushes and block, but they escape into the waters. I roll over and do a pushup into a stand, scamper higher, the shoreline disappearing. A wall of water advances from the north, a creek too high. The face of the man on the bridge goes white. He's frozen in time just a moment, then bends to grab the rope.

I shout, but the roaring water blunts my voice, "Just leave it! Run! Just leave it all behind!" The water so fast, the words too late. The man, along with my bed of ivy, has washed away.

Nothing I came with remains. The bridge has shifted, tipping upcreek, providing for me a near-perfect view of its deck. The burden of the man on the bridge has slid to the edge, hovers over the creek, the weight lugging it overboard with a great splash.

I climb further up the hill. There's a playground two blocks down, close to the school, just past the rose gardens. I remember seeing a drinking fountain somewhere, somewhere near the teeter-totters.

Front Page

covered in the violence of dust the tag
of anonymous cohorts in cahoots with
the destruction of civilization assembly
line ideas mass produced to the lowest
common denominator withholding an
exclusive strain of vital information for
our survival encrypted mystic symbols
deciphered and transcribed by obscure
clandestine sources suspicious covert
contributors to the evil conspiracy of
fossilizing young minds in simulated
choices...

Neon

Anne's biggest fear about the Open House was that nobody would show up and it would be like the night she made all those canapés for her father's Shiva and nobody came. She blocked out that fear and stayed up half the night making brownies off a damn YouTube video and now of course there were ten minutes left of the Open House and sixteen nearly stale brownies because not one person, buyer or moocher, had walked in.

"Screw it," she said and she started eating the brownies. She looked like a raccoon, sitting on the renovated floor hunched over the platter and using both hands to maul the brownies. She burped but she went on. No brownie would get out alive. The more she pictured the liars who promised they'd be there today—that woman with the flavored water at the grocery store, that guy online who wrote in all caps in the middle of the night SAVE ME A BROWNIE ☺—the faster and harder she ate. Her new doctor would be mad. "Widows need to take care of themselves," he said on her last visit. She didn't like the sound of that so she went to her shrink who shrugged: "You lost your husband, Anne. You eat what you want for a while." Anne must have been sugar-stroked because she didn't even hear the woman and the kid come in.

"The door was open," the woman crowed. "So we assumed the house was as well."

Anne hated the way the woman said "as well", as if she were in instructor of some kind but she beamed and licked her teeth and covered her brownie mouth, "You got it. Come on in."

The toddler dove at the platter and pawed at the crumbs. "Mama! Want brownie!"

"Jetson, no. Were those gluten free?"

"I'm afraid not."

The woman sighed and Anne didn't tell her to go fuck herself and her gluten and her kid named *Jetson*. It was times like this that Anne dreamed of throwing on a smock and working at the grocery store stocking shelves. Maybe then she wouldn't hate people so much.

"Would you like a glass of water?"

"Is it tap?"

"Yes."

The woman shook her little head as if Anne suggested a shot of Patron and the husband, because of course there was a husband, walked in. He had a phone attached at his hip and a glistening wedding band and Anne was staring at him. He was irritatingly appealing. He allowed his wife to name their kid *Jetson* yet Anne still felt the hairs on the back of her neck tingle. They weren't gonna buy the house. It wasn't big enough or new enough or anything enough. When they left, Anne waited five minutes before locking up.

* * *

Everyone was going lately so the family at the Open House was no different. Andy had been the first to go. He drove his damn mountain bike off a damn cliff because he liked biking into the stupid great wide open, a place obviously not safe for men in neon bike helmets and bright spandex. Anne always sided with the drivers. Those bike lanes were a fantasy, she argued. There wasn't any room for men like Andy and their bikes. But Andy believed in those lanes, which is why he was dead now. She always told him that neon wouldn't save his life and he always told her she was paranoid and now he was dead so she was right. Her friends circled in the days that followed, offering pies and casseroles, but they were around less and less, they were busy with their own husbands that they loved more now that they saw Anne alone, too young to be old, too old to start over. There are periods in your life when you're a bright gold star on a map that people want to visit. So of course there are periods when you're a yellow DETOUR sign, a place to be avoided. People are not cruel; people are animals. Animals avoid death if they can.

The following Sunday, the husband came back, all bowlegged and summery in tennis whites. She wasn't surprised and she didn't pretend to be surprised that he was here in the not big enough house, no wife, no kid. She stammered on about square footage and skylights. She was back in high school. Flirting as a widow wasn't like flirting as a young single thing. He put his hand on her shoulder, "You can stop now."

She stopped.

"Open your mouth," he said.

She opened her mouth. She closed her eyes even though he didn't tell her to do that. She wanted to be submit.

"You need to floss more," he said. "I think last week's brownies are still in there."

She pulled back and covered her mouth. Stupid Anne. Of course he wasn't hitting on her. She was a hungry widow. A lunatic. He didn't come back for her. Nobody wanted her! What an idiot she was. But then he put his hand on her ass and he kissed her. Smart Anne. Of course he was hitting on her. She was a hungry widow with sugary teeth and he was a disloyal dentist who wanted gluten and sex with someone who didn't name a kid *Jetson*. And so it began, she thought, as banal as a three-bedroom ranch for two and a half baths and granite countertops and a yard big enough for a pool that would never actually have a pool.

* * *

Dr. Eric Paltzen DDS liked driving and so mostly that's what they did. They were outside of LA now, celebrating one month together in his black Lexus with the car seat in the back. He was forty-nine years old and his wife was thirty-four and he told Anne that his marriage was punishment for his ego. He wanted someone young and fertile, a trophy, but she had too much energy and she couldn't remember the seventies and the generation gap broadened more now that they were parents. He wanted to throw Jetson in the back seat and give him a pocket-knife and a bag of cookies and she wanted to teach him Chinese and see to it that nothing delectable ever passed his perfect little lips. So they fought and Anne let him drone on about the fights.

"Only someone young and spoiled can fantasize that a person can live a life without eating a fucking cookie."

"Was she like that before you got married?"

He shrugged. "Not this bad. I mean she always wanted to eat sushi and work out, but that's just par for the course."

Anne tried to lighten things up. "Doesn't she know that her husband is a dentist who can fix all the cavities for free?"

But he didn't laugh. "It's not about his teeth," he corrected her. "It's about the ingredients and the pesticides and the additives making Jet become autistic or fat or disadvantaged physically somehow. But nonetheless, it's out of control."

He corrected her a lot. "Oh, I get it."

On he droned. "It's about keeping his body free of sugar and gluten and fat and everything that tastes good. But you know what I think? I think it's about making him into a pussy. She won't let him play in the yard without a neon bracelet about his peanut allergies."

"Well that seems like a safety precaution."

"He doesn't have a fucking peanut allergy!" Eric roared. "She just doesn't want him to eat fucking peanuts! What the hell kind of a life is that?"

Anne was bored of peanuts and gluten and one good thing about Eric: if she looked out the window he knew to shut up. She let a few minutes pass and he texted while driving. It wouldn't be so terrible to die and Jetson's mom would be pissed for the rest of her life so Anne let it go and stared out at the monotonous desert.

"What a great big block of nothing," she said. "All this land unwanted."

"No," Eric corrected. "This isn't a wasteland or anything like that. There are beautiful trails out here, you just have to know where to go."

"God had a great floor plan," she said, but he didn't laugh. Maybe he knew how badly she wanted him to laugh. He denied her of little things sometimes. But he also gave her little things.

He took his hand off the wheel and she loved his arms and he opened the middle compartment. "I know we said no presents but, I couldn't help myself."

"Oh, Eric," she said. And she felt the way she felt that first day with her eyes closed and her mouth open. He pulled out a little box and put it on her lap. He slammed the compartment shut.

"Happy One Month," he said.

"Ha," she said, which was her standard response when he made a joke she didn't find funny. Her gift was wrapped in kiddy wrapping paper that belonged to Jetson, paper purchased by his damn wife.

Shiny primary-colored puffy cars beamed and beeped and winked and smiled and taunted her: ERIC HAS A FAMILY, YOU WHORE. JETSON HAS FRIENDS AND YOU STOLE THEIR PAPER AND HIS DADDY AND HIS MOM PROBABLY HAS TO GO TO SOME SPECIAL ONLINE BOUTIQUE FOR NATURAL PAPER WITH NO DANGEROUS CHEMICAL DYES THAT COULD SEEP INTO JETSON'S BODY YOU TRESSPASSING GREEDY WIDOW WHORE.

She had no comeback. The cars were right. She remembered when she and Andy found out they couldn't have kids. There was a mound of toys they'd been collecting since they got married, random stuff they found on weekend trips to Temecula or Vegas stuff for the baby they'd have one day when they got around to having a baby. They put the toys in the trunk and drove to The Salvation Army, but Anne couldn't do it.

"It doesn't seem fair," she said to Andy.

He knew her well and he understood and they drove to a dumpster in back of a Friday's restaurant and threw the toys in the trash so that no one else could play with them.

"Sorry about the paper," said Eric. "It's been crazy. But, at least I wrapped it."

"It's fine," she said, because she never told him the way she felt about little things like this. She also thought the air conditioning was too cold and that he braked unnecessarily around trucks and that his taste in music was too feminine but she went along with all of it as she tore into the happy cars, IT'S NOT MY FAULT THAT JETSON'S DADDY MARRIED JETSON'S MOMMY AND MADE JETSON AND IT'S NOT MY FAULT THAT HE DOESN'T WANT TO STAY WITH HER, HER SO THERE! IT'S HER FAULT FOR TURNING INTO AN IDIOT! YOU CAN'T JUST TURN INTO A WHOLE DIFFERENT PERSON AND EXPECT SOMEONE TO KEEP LOVING YOU!

She opened the box. She frowned.

"What's wrong?"

"It's a toothbrush."

"It's electric."

"Eric, it's a toothbrush."

"I want this body of yours to be around for a long time, and those teeth are a part of this body."

She closed the box. She crossed her legs. She tossed the box in the backseat.

"You know, I risk a lot to be with you."

"Do you want a medal?"

"I have a family and a practice and a lot to lose. So really, the only thing you oughta say to me when I risk my ass wrapping a God damn present for you is 'Thank you, Eric. Wow, Eric. I can't believe you're putting your son and your family and your practice on the line for me in addition to taking the time to wrap a present for me'."

"Thank you, Eric."

"You're welcome, Anne."

They were driving now. She was thinking about Andy, which was as stereotypically banal as her affair, as a two-bedroom condo with good light in WeHo. Andy was God now that he was dead. But now Anne was finally remembering all the bad things about her dear, beloved husband. Andy wouldn't consider adoption. He said he'd only love a baby that was "his". Financially, he was a shit, calculating tips on his phone, demanding no ice in his soft drinks, letting her pay for her co-pays when she got sick a few months before they got married and had to go to the doctor over and over again. He went with her. He stood there staring downward with his hands in his pockets but he didn't reach for his credit card and when they went through the CVS drive-thru he let her pay for her prescriptions. He married her. She married him. But he tracked her spending as if she were his teenage daughter and she got mad about that and he swore that he would stop treating her like a kid but there was anger between them, a basic incompatibility where Anne wanted a man to lavish her with gifts and Andy wanted a woman who didn't want gifts, who just wanted to go for a walk or a bike ride.

"You want a bike?" she said one of the first times he mentioned it.

"Yeah, what about you?" he said, staring at the bikes advertised in a Sunday circular.

"I don't like to be on a bicycle."

"How do you know that if you don't try?"

"I hated it when I was little."

"You're not little anymore."

"You buy that bike, it's just going to end up in the basement."

He tore out the page. "Maybe, maybe not. But regardless, this is a damn good deal. I've been tracking the prices and researching and I'm never going to do better than this unless I get a used bike. And for safety reasons, this isn't a time to cut corners. I need a new model and a warranty and all that."

Cheap bastard she thought, figuring he'd go to Sears and deem all the bikes a rip-off. But he didn't. He bought a neon green and black Huffy, and that thing was the gateway drug to bicycle shorts and shaved legs and helmets and creams for his fucking thighs and subscriptions to magazines about bicycles—what is wrong with people?—and trips to *his* doctor because he was choosing to shove his penis into that bicycle seat and what did he think was going to happen to him? His sperm were fine, said the doctor, but Anne knew better. His sperm were scared. They were abused. Of course they didn't want to swim up inside of her! They were angry about being on that fucking bicycle all the time. Who wouldn't hate that?

Sometimes he kept his bicycle helmet on after a ride, sat on the couch with it as if he were a ten-year old boy. She read about this happening to infertile couples. When you can't make a kid, you both turn into kids in your own way. So he became a picky brat, asking waitresses if they had blueberries instead of strawberries and complaining about expired coupons and Anne wanted to crawl under the table, through the kitchen and off to a manly man who wouldn't bristle at adoption or eat berries or wear his helmet indoors or toss it on the floor for her to trip on and argue that anyone who trips over something neon is blind.

"Please, don't cry," said Eric.

"I'm hungry," she said and she stopped crying immediately. Eric was her master; she obeyed.

"We both said things we regret," he said. "We got a good thing, Anne, we do. I'm sorry. And I know you're sorry."

She nodded. She wasn't sorry. Neither was he. Yet everything was fine. She stroked his cheek. He turned on the radio. Now she knew what he really thought of her, that she was the lucky widow, only semi-desirable with bad teeth, unworthy of special wrapping paper, incapable of picking out a toothbrush, stuffed to the gills with gluten and overcooked salmon. She knew who she was. She liked to be pitied, so of course she found someone who would look down on her and correct her and withhold his laughter and she pecked him on the cheek. He patted her on the leg. Good dog. Woof, woof.

They were heading to an overlook where the sunsets with "killer sunsets", and she thought of dead Andy and his useless neon helmet up in heaven, maybe. He wanted Anne to bike with him; he only biked only because she wouldn't bike at all. She pictured him decked out in his electric spandex, laughing off her current indiscretion: *Oh Anne, what are we gonna do with you? I'm dead and still you have to cheat? A married dentist? Not even a doctor!* She could picture him crying: *Anne, you can't do this. What about his family? What about your therapy?* She could see him angry: *You disgust me. I'm gone and you gotta go and tear up a family? You think because you lost me, because you never had kids, you think that gives you a right?*

Everybody loses sometimes, Anne. Get over yourself. Grow the fuck up. She could imagine reaching out to him. She could see him shaking her off, strapping on his helmet, tightening his gloves and mounting his beloved bike —*Anne, there's nothing to say*—riding hard, pumping his legs. If they had a kid, they never would have named it Jetson and he would have stopped riding so much and let his legs get hairy.

To the Girl I Went on a Date With Last Night

Your songs
never got sadder,
how can that
be?
Your mother
still
has your father
you held onto
your God,
I didn't
know
the world
still deserved
something like
that

Yea,
I'll go to brooklyn
I'll pay for the booze
I'll walk you around.
we can stand.
watch
the sun go down
behind
the last projects of lower manhattan.
I'll wonder if I invented you
and I'll wonder if you'll erase me.
i've got the torch in

my hand
don't turn
your face too quickly,
even a breeze
will give the flames
a reason
to dance.

you've got
the after storm blue eyes.
your eyes
tell me you sat on this bench before,
you
know
which two buildings
the sun
will split. it's
the knowledge
of a broken heart.
even with your God
and
your parents
love has been a betrayal.
you spent too much
time on this bench
alone. you
know
the bums,
you know which hipster
will bring the guitar
and what song he
will sing.
you can't know these things
until you're alone. and

you can't
be alone
until you've
learned
you're only safe
with
yourself.

it's hard
to know when
to make a move.
the last light has
attached itself
around your
head
like an
icon.
the divine glow,
whatever
that yellow
ring
is circling the white dove
that means
peace and love
and the sun
and spring
and youth.
i know i should
kiss you now,
but i don't
because
you say
"lets swim to
Manhattan",

and
in the water reflection
I realize I'd rather see you smile
than see
your face touching mine

And maybe
it
should end like that.
with us
not touching
and I could know
you
like the
birds know the sky.
and I won't have to invent you.
and you'll never have to erase me.
your songs
will stay sweet
and we
can share the dark places
of our hearts
that
no one else
gets to see.
i'll
love you
like only a man
who never gets the girl
can,
and every day
will feel like
those
last minutes

we put our heads
to the ground,
figuring out
how to
share our first kiss
goodbye

Fallout: A Response to the Fourth State of Matter

Of all the essays I have read in the last six years, *The Fourth State of Matter* by Jo Ann Beard is probably my favorite, which I revisit annually. This time for the class I am taking called Experimental/Hybrid Forms.

How to do so this time and still learn something more?

I bring it to bed one night and ask my husband if I may read it to him.

Sure, he says, an agreeable man.

I know I am taking a risk with him. He may fall asleep at just the point where he should be paying more attention. He may disappoint me.

I begin.

My reading voice is strong, lyrical. Not monotone, which he dislikes. I have read to him before.

It starts with the collie, and the squirrels. He laughs, often, and I am reassured that he is engaged. I'm enjoying his laughter. I enjoy it often on Sunday mornings with the Times. But sometimes, he perturbs me with his vocalizations. I feel teased into leaving my own reading and asking him "what's so funny." I don't like to be in the dark.

I am enjoying his laughter, too, because I know what is coming. That he will be shocked into silence.

As I read, I notice the short paragraphs stacking up.

My husband loves our cats, but he is truly a dog person. I think of the philosophy that commercials sell more product when there is a dog in them. I think, everyone will love this essay because there are dogs.

The first time I read *The Fourth State of Matter*, I focused on the squirrels. I knew those squirrels, having had a family of squirrels in our house in DC in 1990. I was home on maternity leave and they partied throughout the day somewhere up in the attic. I opened closet after closet looking for them, certain that I would discover a motley crew of goggled creatures sawing and hammering away. When my husband came home at night, they had gone to sleep, and he didn't believe that we needed an exterminator.

I don't really like the part where Jo Ann Beard describes moving the collie's nose like a gearshift in a Maserati. Although, it is more palatable, even cute, on the sixth reading—maybe because I am reading aloud.

When I'm reading, I try not to emphasize the sentences that are foreshadowing, but I feel like I have secret knowledge because I know.

When I read about the husband, I wonder if my husband wonders if I ever thought that way about him. It was almost a coin toss whether we'd stay together after the kids left home, but this year we'll celebrate 27 years. And I've always liked his t-shirts because they reflect a political perspective we share.

I can tell my husband is sorry for the collie.

But I know the collie's misfortune will save the narrator's life.

I love the chalkboard. But it reminds me of 5th grade when Sister Alvernia had wanted to impress a math lesson upon me, one I'd missed because I was sick for a week. I raised my hand, confidently, and went to the blackboard. I was used to getting gold stars and angel stamps on my work and had turned toward her expecting praise. Instead, she smashed my head against my neatly drawn, but incorrect, computation. Chalk dust floated by my eyes.

Of course, I love Chris. And each time I read this essay, I wonder what kind of love Jo Ann really had for Chris. To me, it is more than ambiguous.

I look over at my husband with his eyes closed and begin to feel disappointed. "Are you asleep?" I ask.

"No," he says back.

"Good. This is the 2/3rds point. It's about to get more interesting."

We are all in the rooms and the buildings and the staircases with Gang Lu, although none of us really is. Thank goodness.

Fallout. There is always more fallout than anyone can ever know.

I am choking up as I read, but cover myself pretty convincingly.

A page later, I am crying.

When I read about Chris's mom going back to Germany and quietly killing herself, I think about Columbine, then close by, and the one mom who went to a pawn shop six months later, asked to see a particular gun, loaded it with the bullets she'd brought with her. End of story.

There might be an end to such a story, except there never is.

When I finish reading *The Fourth State of Matter* to my husband, he is very quiet. I am crying over the plasmapause and shards of fly wings, suspended in amber.

"Do you remember this?" I ask. I don't remember 1991 at all, even the war happening.

It is the year my twin brother killed himself, shortly after the new year.

My husband takes out his iPad and Googles shooting, Iowa, November 1, 1991, physicists. He reads silently, then laughs, awkwardly. "Two weeks before, there was another mass murder. That time by truck."

We shake our heads. Sometimes that is all there is.

"Powerful essay," I say, and turn off the lights.

Amphibious

There must be braver ways to be
than this, this holding of cellular secrets
in a stubborn fist. The fat in the knuckles gleams
like moonlight on teeth.

There must be braver ways to be
than a shuffling of each neat part of a life;
a constant sly hiding
to keep things from colliding.

There must be braver ways to be
than the growing of tall tales on demand, the nurturing
of misconceptions, egg-precious,
ripe with the thrill of safety.

Those tadpoles that refuse their budding lungs
and drag their legless forms through the grass –
no double life, no second chance, no new name for them, perhaps
a braver way to be, perhaps.

Old-Fashioned

Her words came straight from the lungs, barely shaped
and the sound put me in mind
of a lovesick snake.
Nice girls blocked out the bad words with stars, an image
romantic enough, if you thought of them glittering;
fierce enough, if you thought of them burning.

Kindling

As Maggie tapped her toes on the carpeted floor of her doctor's office she thought about the day her dead husband used jazz hands in a morning conversation they had over coffee and toast.

"Celia got a job interview for next week," he said, stirring sugar into his cup. "Supposed to be at that Roberson Theater with the terrible seats."

"What's the job?" Maggie asked.

He spread his fingers, shook his wrists—jazz hands.

"Stage hand."

Maggie frowned, biting into her toast thirty years ago and tapping her foot in Dr. Beale's waiting room now. It was a bad job, a bad position.

The door to the sacrosanct hallways of the doctor's office clicked open and a young woman with a clipboard leaned out.

"Margaret Coulson?"

Maggie popped out of her seat and bobbed after the woman down the hall.

"Just a routine follow-up, right?" the woman asked. She pulled open the exam room door and ushered Maggie inside.

"Yes," said Maggie. "Just making sure it heals right."

She held up her finger and the splint glinted in the fluorescent light. Maggie blinked it away and thought about the heavy oak desk her husband used to pay bills for twenty years, now lying in several pieces in the attic of her home. After struggling and heaving it up the stairs in her effort to remove any hint, any reminder of any life before her husband's death, one of its legs slipped off a step and pinned her index finger against the wall with a drawer.

"Son of a bitch." Maggie heaved the desk away from the wall and kicked it back down the stairs. "Motherfucking son of a bitch." The desk creaked, slamming into the ground and popping a knob off the cabinet.

She swept out the back door and returned with the hatchet from her shed. Using her good hand she chopped the desk into pieces and threw them into the attic before going to the hospital.

"Just trying to clean up the house," she told the nurse as the woman unhooked her splint with slow, methodical precision. "Just wanted a tidy home and look what happens."

The nurse smiled and shook her head. "It always does." The large freckle on her nose sashayed through the air as she stepped back to the door. "Stay put and the doctor will be here in a moment."

Maggie's eyes followed her freckle through the closed door, down the hall, to the front desk, into the break room. That was Celia's freckle—her niece the stage hand named for Maggie's mother. The size of a bluebottle, that freckle. The only vivid memory from Maggie's prim and proper childhood, that freckle.

"Fix your collar, young lady. You look like a harlot."

"Pull your hair back, young lady. You look like a harlot."

"Don't walk with those girls home from school anymore, young lady. They're harlots."

"Of course we can't spare you in the afternoons, young lady. People who work at the Roberson are harlots."

A bad job, a bad position. Maggie tried to bend her index finger. It was stiff and the knuckle cracked. She was tapping her toes again when the doctor walked in.

"All right—let's see here," Dr. Beale said, rolling over a chair and plopping his clipboard onto the exam bed. The paper crinkled and sighed.

Dr. Beale inspected Maggie's finger. His warm hands caressed hers like a calloused masseuse. She imaged him using a push mower on his lawn.

"I think you're all set," he said, standing and adjusting his white coat. "Healed great—just be careful moving furniture from now on. Try to get some help with those sorts of things, Mrs. Coulson."

Maggie tilted her head. "It's not very flexible," she said. "Is that okay?"

"Oh, sure. It'll take a few more weeks for it to feel completely back to normal. But not too long. You'll be dancing in no time." He spread his fingers, shook his wrists—jazz hands.

Maggie grabbed two hard candies from the front desk on her way out. She ate candy like she read books: without patience. As soon as she got in the car she popped both candies in her mouth, sucked for ten seconds, and then chomped them into sticky goo that stuck to her teeth. Life was too short to savor Jolly Ranchers. She'd been reading books the same way since she was sixteen: start in the middle, read to the end, and then go back to the beginning until she got to where she started. Life was too short for rising action. Maggie was all denouement.

She passed the Roberson Theater on her left and thought of her husband and his breakfast jazz hands, about nose freckles on nurses. At least nursing was a proper profession, a respectable job. Maggie frowned again, crunching away on Dr. Beale's hard candy as she drove to a house completely emptied of furniture on the first floor but stuffed like a teddy bear with chopped up bits of desks and beds on the second.

Continuum

Did Ludwig van Beethoven
dream he was a music critic
whose impatience insisted,
The crescendo is impertinent
and must be allowed to growl in full force,
never to be muted like the song of a sparrow?

Did Nathanial Hawthorne
dream of crawling inside word-houses
full of nuances and guilt?
Did his eyes seek
the deepest darkness
exposing both history and hope?

Did Gustave Moreau
paint his dreams?
And if he did, did he whisper,
I will live forever
in a world of intricate ideas,
designs, and colors?

Did Sigmund Freud
dream while sleeping
on a park bench,
where icy snow gathered
around his body?
Was he mumbling,
I understand,

I understand?

Did Albert Einstein
dream the death of time as he
rode in a continuum
while repeating,
Time is nothing like the tiny steps we take
when we believe in the linear?

Did James Baldwin
identify with hungry sparrows,
houses designed with words and
darkened windows,
dreams, and the forever
color of snow-cold yearnings,
ideas, and designs?
Did he understand the fear
of sleeping in the cupped hands of tomorrow
while recognizing the death of time?

Did he dream of wearing a white suit,
a white shirt, and a bloodied heart?

The Bee

The Father
The note's folded in half under an electric bill on the kitchen table. It could be just another one of Katherine's scraps. Shopping lists, obscure reminders—*lanterns, I hate my F, get dog food* (we don't have a dog)—all scribbled on the pages of expensive travel mags. This one, barely legible in navy blue over the right half of a navy blue pagoda, says *IMPORTANT!! Girls' Night!! Don't forget to pick up Jayson from soccer!!!!* I swat a bee with the note and slide it back under the unopened electricity bill. The bee alights on the window sill and sits there like it's chosen a peaceful death.

The Mother
My biggest dream? *Beijing* I write in the ironically tiny gap *Cosmopolitan* has left for me. My biggest disappointment? I write a fat enigmatic *F* because I can always say I meant *figure* or *face* or, if I'm feeling near-honest, *friendships*. Why don't I just write FAMILY in enormous red letters, drain my savings and disappear?

Jayson's holding out his spoon for more Count Chocula. I'll never be done feeding him. When I'm 80 and he's 68, he'll still be holding out that spoon. At twelve, he'll never be older than four. Sometimes he wants the whole box, and sometimes I just let him eat it. Sometimes his teachers call and leave messages on my voicemail: 'Mrs. Webb, if you get this message, come pick up Jayson. He's climbing the walls. We're afraid of him.' I don't answer the phone on these days.

'Beijing,' I say and show Jayson the brochure. 'You know where that is, Honeybee?' And Jayson says, 'Out there?' 'That's right, BeeBee,' I say.

'Out there where Mommy never gets to go.' I hold up my hands like I'm peeking through prison bars. Jayson laughs, and I wish I knew whether he got the joke. I tear off half a brochure page with the least writing and write in big blue letters *IMPORTANT!! Girls' Night!! Don't forget to pick up Jayson from soccer!!!!* Tyler is still sleeping because, in his own words, 'It's not my fucking turn to feed the Bee.'

The Father

After work. Nachos and margaritas until we puke. The note is pinned to my cubicle right on my poster of Pamela Anderson—right on the money, like I'm blind if I don't see it, right? And why shouldn't I see it? It's not like the guys wrote the note blue on blue, then folded and buried it under my files, right? Katherine never wanted me to see the note to pick up Jayson in the first place. So now we pull out the big guns. Watch my moves. They don't teach this stuff in couples counselling. I'm gonna force the blow-out argument, the one where we scream at each other about who's sabotaging this family more until one of us raises a hand. We'll both threaten to call child services, blame each other for Jayson's disability, and then have sex.

The Mother

Tyler's toast is stiff and cold when I tiptoe into the bedroom to shake him—but not hard enough to wake him. If he oversleeps one more time, he'll lose his job and maybe this house, which will give me an excuse to divorce him. I'll deem him a loser: an irresponsible 34-year-old kid. I'll leave him loudly, throw the prison doors open, fly to Beijing the same day and find a job working in an American steak restaurant teaching grinning Chinese people how to eat with a knife and fork. My arc toward freedom will be that easy. I'll dye my hair blond to be exotic and I'll speak Chinese with an affected nasal accent like they expect from exotic Americans. And at night—I don't know— I'll do whatever the fuck I want, won't I?

The Bee

I'm playing soccer on the soccer field. The Mother says a soccer field is "an unimaginable expanse," but it is also like a playpen with its lines and grown-ups watching. It's framed with lines like an electric fence, like prison bars. The Father says I'm crap at soccer, which is true, but I can buzz behind the other boys and two girls like they have honey, which is the best thing in the world.

If the ball hits my foot, I have to kick it to someone wearing the same color as me, which is blue today. Coach Tim has told me this exactly four times but keeps saying he's said it a million times, which isn't possible. Blue is darker than yellow. A lot darker. I kick the ball when I trip on it and the mothers and fathers on the outside of the prison playpen bars scream *Get up, Jayson!* Coach Tim hollers *Blue Jayson Blue!*—which counts as one more time, not two.

The Father's name is Tyler Webb and The Mother's name is Katherine Webb. If they're late picking me up again, I should *alert* people because there are mean men out there where Mommy never gets to go. I don't like to *alert* people. Their cars smell funny, like cat dodo or chicken soup or hair. I like walking home because I like the cold air on my cheeks and I like being a bee finding home, like there's something inside me that just knows.

I live at 1123 Elk Trail—not circle or bend or ridge, which are all nearby but I don't live on any of these—and I can walk to 1123 Elk Trail from here because I know what the signs mean. I know that Elk has three letters and Trail has more, and I know where The Mother keeps the spare key. And I know if The Father and The Mother aren't there when I get home, I have to sit quietly in the kitchen and wait.

I Live in Ernest

First, a moveable feast
Lost in Paris
Olives, goujon, crusty bread.
Then the manuscript
Terse, filled with meaning
Sentences taut
like lariat tails
Leave people behind
with trace marks
on a fence.
I live in Ernest.
Rifle to my head or heart
Good stiff drink
and morning air.
I live in alleys
on mountaintops
and ski
with the vigor of a body double.
Oysters slide down
a welcome throat
Flowers smell fleeting
Time is short and
sweet as a whiff
in an orangerie.
I live tapping code
from a cave
Alive

Here
Waiting.
I live in Ernest.

AUTHORS

Christopher Allen
Christopher Allen is the author of "Conversations with S. Teri O'Type (a Satire)," an episodic adult cartoon about a man struggling with expectations. Allen's award-winning fiction has appeared, or is forthcoming, in *Indiana Review, SmokeLong Quarterly's Best of the First Ten Years anthology, Prime Number Magazine, A-Minor Magazine, Blue Fifth Review* and *Pure Slush*, among many others. A finalist at *Glimmer Train* in 2011, Allen has been nominated for *Best of the Net* and the *Pushcart Prize* twice. He is the managing editor of the daily litzine *Metazen* and lives in Germany.

Molly Bonovsky Anderson
Molly Bonovsky Anderson grew up in Saint Cloud, Minnesota. She studied Philosophy, Art History, and English at Northern Michigan University. Her work has appeared in *Crab Orchard Review, Passages North, Penduline Press, Big Fiction, Wilde Magazine, Breakwater Review, Burrow Press Review,* and other print and online journals. She lives in Upper Michigan with her husband and son, and is the fiction editor at *Pithead Chapel* magazine.

Carol Bell
After studying biology and chemistry at the University of Colorado, Carol Bell worked for many years as a pharmaceutical chemist. Once retired, she chose to abandon her life of analysis, gas chromatographs and titrations to live on a hay ranch on the Western Slope of Colorado where she could focus on writing poetry, short stories and non-fiction. She studied at Colorado Mesa University in Grand Junction, Colorado where she earned a degree in English. She has studied with Colette Inez, Christopher Merrill, Amy Irvine, Dr. Barry Laga, and Craig Childs. Her work has appeared in *Amarillo Bay, Bayou, The Broome Review, California Quarterly, Cape Rock, Forge, Mobius, Pilgrimage Magazine, RiverSedge, Soundings East, Studio One,* and *Talking River* among others. Her first non-fiction book, "Soldier # 37483425; Memories of WWII," will be available in book stores soon.

Rose Mary Boehm

A German-born UK national, Rose Mary Boehm lives and works in Lima, Peru. Author of two novels and a poetry collection ("TANGENTS"), her poems have appeared or are forthcoming in US poetry reviews. *Toe Good Poetry, Poetry Breakfast, Burning Word, Muddy River Review, Pale Horse Review, Pirene's Fountain, Other Rooms, Requiem Magazine, Big River Review, Full of Crow, Poetry Quarterly, Punchnel's, Avatar, Verse Wisconsin, Naugatuck River Review, Boston Literary, Red River Review, Ann Arbor, Main Street Rag, Misfit Magazine* and others.

Melanie J. Cordova

Melanie J. Cordova is currently a PhD student in Creative Writing Fiction at Binghamton University. She has stories out or forthcoming with *Red Savina Review, Whitefish Review, The Oklahoma Review, Yamassee,* and various others. Melanie also serves as Editor-in-Chief to *Harpur Palate* and as Coordinator of *Writing By Degrees 2014.*

Chris Crittenden

Chris Crittenden lives in a remote area of Maine and has a PhD in philosophy. His latest book of poetry is "Escape From the Orchard of Wheels," which is nearing a deal with *Medulla Review Publishing.*

Janet Frishberg

Janet Frishberg lives and writes in a light blue room in San Francisco. She's currently editing her first book, a memoir. You can find her work in *Literary Orphans, Cease, Cows, sparkle & blink, the SF Chronicle,* and soon in *The Rufous City Review, r.kv.r.y quarterly,* and *Black Heart Magazine.*

Khanh Ha

Khanh Ha's debut novel is "FLESH" (2012, *Black Heron Press*). A three-time Pushcart nominee and a two-time Best of the Net Award nominee, his work has appeared or is forthcoming in *Waccamaw Journal, storySouth, Greensboro Review, Saint Ann's Review, Permafrost Magazine, DUCTS, Lunch Ticket, Yellow Medicine Review,* and other fine journals.

Eileen Hennessy

Eileen Hennessy lives in and loves New York City. She is a translator of foreign-language documentation and books on art history into English from several other West European languages, and an adjunct associate professor in the Translation Studies program at New York

University. Her poems and short stories have been published in numerous literary journals, including *Confluence, The New York Quarterly, Paintbrush, The Paris Review, Western Humanities Review,* and others. "This Country of Gale-force Winds," a collection of her poems, was published by *NYQ Books* in 2011.

Nancy Hightower

Nancy Hightower's short fiction and poetry has been published in *Word Riot, storySouth, The New York Quarterly, Gargoyle, Prick of the Spindle,* and *Prime Number Magazine,* among others. Her eco-fantasy novel, "Elementarí Rising," was published by *Pink Narcissus Press* in 2013.

Lizzy Huitson

Lizzy Huitson is a writer of poetry and short fiction, and has been published in a number of literary journals and magazines including *The Waterhouse Review, GlassFire Magazine, Vine Leaves Literary Journal* and *Fiction365.* She has also published an ebook of poetry, titled "Honeycomb Bones". She keeps trying (and failing) to write a detective novel.

Caroline Kepnes

Caroline Kepnes is a native Cape Codder and Brown University graduate who splits her time between Los Angeles and Massachusetts. During her sophomore year of high school, she earned an honorable mention in Sassy Magazine's (best magazine ever) Fabulous Fiction Contest. Her stories have most recently appeared in *Drunk Monkeys, Eclectica, Necessary Fiction* and *Two Serious Ladies.* She has contributed to *Entertainment Weekly, E! Online* and *Yahoo! TV.* She has written episodes of "7th Heaven" and "The Secret Life of the American Teenager." She completed a novel for *Alloy Entertainment* that will be published in 2014. Her debut short film "Miles Away" will soon hit the festival circuit as well.

Loren Kleinman

Loren Kleinman is a young, American-born poet with roots in New Jersey. She has a B.A. in English Literature from Drew University and an M.A. in Creative and Critical Writing from the University of Sussex (UK). Her poetry has appeared in literary journals such as *Nimrod, Wilderness House Literary Review, Writer's Bloc, Journal of New Jersey Poets, Paterson Literary Review (PLR), Resurgence (UK), HerCircleEzine* and

Aesthetica Annual. She was the recipient of the *Spire Press Poetry Prize* (2003), was a 2000 and 2003 *Pushcart Prize* nominee, and was a 2004 *Nimrod/Pablo Neruda Prize* finalist for poetry. In 2003, *Spire Press* (NYC) published her first collection of poetry "Flamenco Sketches", which explored the relationship between love and jazz. Her second collection of poetry, "The Dark Cave Between My Ribs," is due to release in 2014 (*Winter Goose Publishing,* 2014).

Scott Laudati
Scott Laudati lives in Brooklyn with his boxer, Satine. Visit him at www.ScottLaudati.com.

Sarah Lilius
Sarah Lilius currently lives in Arlington, VA. Some places her work can be found include the *Denver Quarterly, Court Green, BlazeVOX,* and *Bluestem.* Her website is www.sarahlilius.com.

Bruce Makous
His first novel, "Riding the Brand," (*Hilliard & Harris,* 2004) was covered in *The Wall Street Journal* for its controversial illustration of how the high-tech venture capital industry was operated like organized crime. *The Charlotte Observer* said Riding the Brand "provides that needed hook." Richard Burgin, editor of *Boulevard,* the award-winning literary journal, said, "In Riding the Brand, his debut novel, Bruce Makous shows his masterful skill in bringing to life lovable but sinister characters in a fiercely competitive high-tech world." His second novel, "Virtually Dead," was released in 2006. He has active member status with *Mystery Writers of America,* and serves as a fundraiser for the *ACLU.*

Steven Minchin
Steven Minchin is a poet, painter and video artist in upstate New York's cultural capital, Albany. He has recently published his 50th poem and is finishing work on the upcoming book "Eleven Perditions After Love and Other Nauseating Adventures." His work has appeared in *Mad Swirl, Short, Fast and Deadly,* as well as *vox poetica* and others.

Beth Smelser Nelson

Beth Smelser Nelson's writing has appeared in *American Literary Review* and *Camera Arts Magazine*. She's been awarded residencies at Jentel, The Hill House, and Brush Creek Ranch. Beth has trekked in Nepal, gone on photo safari in Kenya, and tramped the backwoods of New Zealand. She and her husband David once lived as expatriates in Saudi Arabia, and later, parented a foster child. Beth lives in Centennial, Colorado and is working on her short story collection, "Rurality." Her blog "You've Got to Start Someplace" is available at Wordpress.

Kevin Oaks

Kevin Oaks, originally from the North East, is currently surviving the unconventional vortex of creativity also known as Venice Beach, CA. His obsession with language games and word play drive him to pursue the dream of being a writer and embrace the reality of becoming a book. "Front Page" is a selection from "Better Luck Next Time" that explores the illusion of free will.

Catherine Arturi Parilla

Catherine Arturi Parilla's poetry has appeared in *The Alembic, Compass Rose, descant, Eclipse, Green Hills Literary Lanter, Knightscapes, Pisgah Review, Poem,* and *Wisconsin Review.* Presently, she is working on her manuscript "Shadows Lie." For three years, she had been a poetry reader for *YARN,* an internet network for young adult literature. Her academic writing includes her book "A Theory for Reading Dramatic Texts: A Reading of Luigi Pirandello and Garcia Larca." A professor at Fairleigh Dickinson University, she teaches creative and expository writing and resides in Alpine, NJ.

James Peters

James Peters was born in Lancaster, PA in 1971. He's lived in the breathtaking front range of the Rocky Mountains just outside of Denver for almost 20 years. He's been selling real estate for over a decade. Yet, now in his 40's, he chooses to devote more of his time to his lovely wife, Jen, his wonderful daughter, Kara, and to his writing, just for the joy of it.

Aleksander Plonski

Aleksander Plonski was born in Poland in 1977 where he grew up, benefitting from the excellent education provided by the communist regime. By 1992, when he emigrated to the USA, he was already inspired by many of the British and American writers such as Blake, Whitman and Kerouac among many others. Since his arrival in Brooklyn, he has dedicated himself to the mastery of the written English language which culminated, in a way, when he graduated with honors in Philosophy and Literature in 2000. An author of innumerable poems and short stories he never pursued publication as much as the adventure of life. His story continues in Buenos Aires where he currently resides mending his broken heart and raising his 9 year old son. If you were to ask him, he would say that he was much more proud of surviving all the fucked up things he's done than of anything he had written - but then again, it's only the beginning.

David Press

David Press lives in Milwaukee where he has taught, run an educational publishing company, sold battery-operated Santa Clauses, and authored six young adult nonfiction books on abolitionists, environmentalists, and such. These days, David writes genre busting micro novels of overlapping, contradictory and non linear nano episodes. Some of these may be read in *Fiction Fix, Fringe, Red Fez, Cobalt, Burdock* and elsewhere. Press also writes thirty minute, theater of the bizarre plays, most recently a one actor about Arthur Miller, Joe DiMaggio, and the ghost of Marilyn Monroe. He counts the Brothers Grimm and David Milch among his posse of influencers. Active in the Milwaukee arts and open mic communities, Press lives with his wife, Petra, an art teacher, printmaker and book artist whose works are exhibited nationally. They have collaborated on a series of 'zines and a postcard novel.

Adam "Bucho" Rodenberger

Adam "Bucho" Rodenberger is a 34 year old writer from Kansas City living in San Francisco. He holds dual Bachelor's degrees in Philosophy & Creative Writing and completed his MFA in Writing at the University of San Francisco in 2011. He has been published in *Alors, Et Tois?, Agua Magazine, Offbeatpulp, Up The Staircase, The Gloom Cupboard, BrainBox Magazine, Cause & Effect Magazine, the Santa Clara Review,*

Penduline Press, Aphelion, Glint Literary Journal, Bluestem Magazine, and *Phoebe.*

Jon Sindell
A human, Jon Sindell earns his bread as a fulltime personal humanities tutor. He curates the *Rolling Writers* reading series in San Francisco, and practiced law once't. His short fiction has appeared or will appear in dozens of publications, including *Hobart, Pithead Chapel, Word Riot, Zouch, New South, Prick Of The Spindle, Switchback, Weave,* and *Beatdom.* His baseball–plus novel, "The Mighty Roman," is a wild ride to the manly heart of baseball.

Matt Staley
Matt Staley is a graduate student at Western New Mexico University. When he's not lost on the Appalachian Trail or slinging snakes out of his kayak on some rancid river, Matt is writing poetry and flash fiction. His most recent work appeared in *The Bitchin' Kitsch.* Matt is currently an Assistant Editor with the *Red Savina Review,* and he lives in Myrtle Beach, SC.

Xenia Taiga
Xenia Taiga's work is in *Four Way Review, Litro, Storm Cellar Quarterly, Eastlit* and other beautiful places. She lives in southern China with a cockatiel and an Englishman.

Tamar Telian
Tamar Telian is a Long Beach-based writer. Her work has appeared in *So to Speak, Carnival, The Mary Sue, Side B Magazine,* and *Pearl.* She believes cats are our future—teach them well and let them lead the way.

Barbara Tramonte
Barbara Tramonte is a professor at the School for Graduate Studies, SUNY Empire State College and has had poems published in many literary magazines.

Howard Winn
"My writing, both fiction and poetry, has been published by such journals as *Dalhousie Review, Taj Mahal Review* (India), *Galway Review* (Ireland), *Descant* (Canada), *Antigonish Review, Southern Humanities Review,*

Chaffin Review, Thin Air Literary Journal, and *Futures Trading Literary Journal.* I am presently working on a novel dealing with Tom Brokaw's 'Greatest Generation.' My B. A. is from Vassar College. I have an M.A. in Creative Writing from Stanford University . I have done additional graduate work at the University of California San Francisco. My doctoral work was done at N. Y. U. I been a social worker in California and currently am a faculty member of SUNY as Professor of English.

Lia Woodall

Lia Woodall is an emerging nonfiction writer living in Denver, Colorado with her husband and three cats. She is a member of *Lighthouse Writers Workshop* and a charter member of *Salon Denver.* Her first essay, "Torn in Two," was nominated for a *Pushcart Prize* and can be found in Vol. 15 of *South Loop Review: Creative Nonfiction + Art* (Oct. 2013). Her second essay, "The Scream" was awarded 2nd place by *Sonora Review* in its 2013 Essay Contest and is forthcoming in Issue 64 (March 2014). She doesn't currently have a twitter account, but she can take shorthand dictation. Thanks, Mrs. Witcher.

This anthology is generously sponsored by Outskirts Press

Visit www.crackthespine.com to subscribe to our weekly digital magazine or to review our submission guidelines.

www.ingramcontent.com/pod-product-compliance
Lightning Source LLC
Chambersburg PA
CBHW070555180626
46817CB00005B/1845

9780988978256